# A SCANDALOUS KISS

Without so much as a by your leave, Adam left his place on the opposite side of the inglenook and joined Marianne on the other carved bench, sitting very close to her. She still held the little gold acorn between her fingers, and he put his hand beneath hers, letting the trinket rest in his palm.

Even with him sitting so close to her, Marianne might have retained her composure had the back of Adam's large, very masculine hand not rested against her throat. At the feel of his warm flesh touching hers, all coherent thought vanished from her mind. Unfortunately, her ladylike inhibitions disappeared as well—those inhibitions that were supposed to keep females from experiencing wanton feelings—and Marianne found herself leaning toward Adam, her face lifted to his. . . .

Books by Martha Kirkland

THE GALLANT GAMBLER
THREE FOR BRIGHTON
THE NOBLE NEPHEW
THE SEDUCTIVE SPY
A GENTLEMAN'S DECEPTION
THAT SCANDALOUS HEIRESS

Published by Zebra Books

# THAT
# SCANDALOUS
# HEIRESS

*Martha Kirkland*

Zebra Books
Kensington Publishing Corp.

http://www.zebrabooks.com

*For the forty-niners of Marshall County
High School, Guntersville, AL.
Congratulations on your fiftieth reunion.*

ZEBRA BOOKS are published by

Kensington Publishing Corp.
850 Third Avenue
New York, NY 10022

Copyright © 2000 by Martha Kirkland

First Printing: May, 2000
10 9 8 7 6 5 4 3 2 1

Printed in the United States of America

# Prologue

*Hampstead Heath*
*June 1819*

The craggy-faced physician rubbed his hand across his sleep-swollen eyelids, ignoring the raindrops that clung to the curled brim of his sodden hat. Dragged from the warmth of his bed far too early, he glowered at first one man then at the other. In no humor to suffer fools, he said, "My lords, is there no way this dispute can be settled without bloodshed?"

"No," Lord Worley replied, his flat, pug-dog face rendered even less appealing than usual by the hatred in his pale blue eyes. "I demand satisfaction."

The physician turned to the taller, younger man. "What of you, Lord Jenson? You are aware, are you not, that dueling has been outlawed? Is there nothing I can say to dissuade you from your course?"

Adam Jenson, the seventh Viscount Jenson, was well over six feet tall and accustomed to looking down upon his fellow man; from his vantage point, he stared coldly at the shorter, stockier Lord Worley. "This meeting," he informed the doctor, "is none of my doing. Lord Worley has only to apologize for his ill-advised remark, and I will be happy to adjourn to the nearest inn, where I

will stand the entire party gathered to a meal and un
limited bottles of *mein* host's finest brandy."

"Apologize!" Lord Worley spat upon the ground to
show his contempt for such a plan, then he tossed his
head back to dislodge a lock of damp blond hair that
had fallen across his forehead. "I'll see you in hell
first!"

The physician sighed. "As you wish, my lords." After
gazing into the grayness of the dawn sky, a sky that
gave little promise of sunshine that day, he turned to
the two men chosen as seconds to the combatants. "In
ten minutes, gentlemen, there should be enough light to
allow this madness to commence. Until then, take the
principals aside and see if you can talk some sense into
them."

Lord Worley and his second turned and walked to the
right. At the same time, Mr. Franklin Llewellyn clutched
at the sleeve of the corbeau evening coat worn to perfection by his boyhood friend, urging Adam Jenson toward a stand of yew trees some distance to the left.
"Over there," he said, his voice a blend of anger and
frustration.

Viscount Jenson was a good three inches taller than
his friend and outweighed him by at least two stone,
but he allowed himself to be led across the soggy
ground to the yews. Though Franklin was two years
younger than Adam's thirty-one years, the two had been
inseparable since their days at Harrow, and if Adam Jenson would listen to anyone—which was doubtful—it
would be Franklin.

Once they reached the still-dripping branches of the
yews, where a degree of privacy was possible, Franklin
looked up into the hard-edged, yet handsome face of
his friend. In the gathering dawn, raindrops glistened

on Adam's short, thick black hair; meanwhile, his near-black eyes stared ahead coldly, almost as if the thought of impending death meant nothing to him.

"This is insanity, Adam. Surely you know that Worley has the best record at Manton's shooting gallery."

"I am aware of his skill."

"Then let me see what I can do to get him to take back his words. Please. It is not as if anyone at White's believed for a minute that you had cheated during that final rubber. As if you needed to! Why, no one can best you at whist, and the entire town knows it."

The viscount shook his head. "Worley's anger has nothing to do with last evening's card play."

"Then, what the deuce has it—"

"Playing cards with me, then accusing me of cheating, was but part of a well-laid plan to conceal his true reason for wishing to put an end to my existence."

"His true reason for wishing—" Franklin stopped abruptly then drew a steadying breath. "And that reason is?"

"Worley has disliked me for some time, but I believe his wish to kill me took root several days ago, when he got his first glimpse of his new son and heir."

"His heir?" Franklin raked his hand through his hair, his frustration growing. "I do not see the connection."

"Then, you must be the only person in town who has not heard the rumor."

After muttering an oath, he said, "Fiend seize it, Adam, if you keep me in suspense a moment longer, I vow I shall call you out myself."

Though Adam smiled at his friend's threat, the action was but a slight lifting of the corners of his mouth. The smile vanished almost as soon as it appeared, the first hint that he was not as calm as he would have Franklin believe. "Rumor has it that Lord and Lady Worley, both of whom are blue-eyed blonds, are the proud parents of a newborn with black hair and brown eyes."

"Damnation!"

"As you say. Unfortunately, her ladyship's husband has taken it into his head that *I* am the father of his heir."

Franklin lowered his voice. "Are you?"

The viscount offered no reply, merely lifted one imperious eyebrow, giving his friend the sort of cold stare that had been known to make lesser men tremble in their boots.

"Sorry, old fellow. No wish to offend. However, it is common knowledge that Lady Worley pursued you relentlessly last season."

"I gave her no encouragement."

"You don't need to. Never have. Not even when the ladies are as beautiful as Beatrice Worley."

"Damn her beauty! I wanted none of the vixen before she sold herself to a man old enough to be her father, and I wanted even less to do with her after she wed Worley."

"Then, why does Worley believe you to be the father of the child?"

A muscle twitched in Adam's tightly clenched jaw. "He believes it because Beatrice managed to corner me once last August, at Lord Sheffly's house party."

"Never say so!"

"It was the night of the ball, and I, bored to near madness by the machinations of Sheffly's wife and the simpering of his hen-witted daughter, was so foolish as to wander into the gentleman's library, alone." He laughed, though the sound had no humor in it. "Unfortunately, the rapacious Lady Worley followed me into the softly lit book room, and as luck would have it, she had succeeded in wrapping her arms around my neck, when her husband opened the door."

"Damnation! That was in August, you say?"

"August thirty-first, to be exact."

After counting back on his fingers, Franklin gasped. "Egod! Nine full months. Bad timing, that."

"An understatement, my friend."

Franklin glanced back over his shoulder to that spot where Lord Worley and his second stood. "Perhaps if I explained the situation to Worley, he would—"

"Call you a fool. Or worse." Adam shook his head. "This is one time, I fear, when my reputation carries more weight than my word. But I beg of you, Franklin, do not say 'I told you so.' Though it would be nothing more than the truth, I wish you would resist the temptation to remind me how many times you have warned me of just such a possibility as this."

Ignoring his friend's attempt at levity, Franklin said, "What if Worley gets off the first shot? With his skill, he could easily—"

"Gentlemen!" the physician called. "The ten minutes are accomplished. If you have not succeeded in talking sense into the principals, please come forward and see to the loading of the pistols."

Franklin Llewellyn stared into Adam's face for a moment, searching his brain for some word that would convince his friend to turn and walk away. When he found no such word, he took the proffered hand and shook it, holding to it overlong, his emotions making him shake from head to toe. Not surprisingly, Adam's hand felt steadier than his own, and Franklin had to will himself to stop trembling. In his capacity as second, it was his duty to load the pistol, and he had no wish to make a costly mistake.

While he approached the physician, who held open a slender mahogany case that housed the two ivory-handled dueling pistols as well as the powder flask and measure, the linen bag of bullets, and the mallet for starting the bullet into the barrel, Franklin removed his handkerchief and wiped his damp palms upon the linen. Without another word, he chose one of the short-barreled pistols, then he stepped back and waited while the other second loaded the remaining weapon.

Once both weapons were loaded, the physician called to the principals. "My lords. Come forward, if you please, and take a position, back-to-back."

Being careful not to press the spring that would set off the hair trigger, Franklin walked over to Adam and handed him the loaded pistol. "Adam, please. I—"

"Get out of the way, Frank. If it is to be, I am prepared to go to hell this day. I am not, however, prepared to watch my best friend bleed to death because he stood too close to me during an idiotic duel."

As if in a trance, Franklin moved away, and the duelers took a position with their backs to each other, their weapons cocked and pointed toward the sky. Following the rules of the *code duello,* the two men took ten paces forward. They moved slowly, purposefully, the only sound the slight *squishing* of their boots upon the wet earth.

When the paces were measured off, both men stopped.

"On my count," the physician said, "you may turn and fire at will. Are you ready?"

"Ready," Lord Worley said, unfolding the lapels of his coat to conceal the white of his shirt and cravat.

"Ready," Viscount Jenson replied, unfolding the corbeau lapels as well.

The physician cleared his throat. "One. Two. Three. Turn."

Both men turned, taking a sideways pose to offer the least target, then they straightened their arms so the pistols were on a line with their faces. Lord Worley moved first, taking one small step forward. Unfortunately, it was a misstep, for the heel of his right boot touched not solid ground but a clump of wet grass, and his foot skittered out from under him. Unable to maintain his balance, he fell to his left knee, his pistol firing as he fell.

A split second following the loud report of the pistol fire, Adam recoiled slightly and clutched his right side. A dark liquid began to ooze from between his fingers, the source of the flow hidden beneath his waistcoat.

When Franklin would have rushed to his friend's aid, the physician caught his arm and held him back. "You may fire at will," the doctor said once again.

Lord Worley, his face filled with rage, rose to his feet, then tossed aside the spent pistol. As he turned to glower at the viscount, he folded back the lapels of his coat, exposing his white-shirted chest. "Even you cannot miss," he said, his words defiant. "Shoot, you bastard!"

Adam gave him look for look, the tension between the two men filling the damp air, then he lifted his pistol above his head and shot straight up into the gray dawn sky.

# One

Marianne McCord held on to the rail of the canal boat as it entered the final lock. Still fascinated by the procedure, she leaned forward so she might watch the canalman turn the massive crank that opened the single gate at the top of the chamber. The instant the gate was open, the sluices began emptying the water, and for the next twenty minutes the barge sank lower and lower until it reached the bottom of the chamber and passed through the double gates into the Derwent River.

During the five minutes needed for the barge to draw up alongside a massive wooden dock, the fascinated passenger studied the water beneath her where the grayish stone buildings of the small village were reflected on the surface of the busy river. Beyond the village was a deep valley of dark green woods, and in the far distance, stretching almost to the sky, were the high crags. The view was a study in shades of green and gray, and Marianne loved it on sight.

So this was the Peak District.

Having lived the past nine of her nearly twenty-six years in Wales, she was accustomed to spectacular scenery, but this scenery was different—this scenery was now *hers*. She had gone to Wales against her will—an orphan with no voice in her own future—but she had come to Derbyshire willingly, gladly, hoping to begin a new life.

The trip from Wales had needed four full days to complete. It had begun on the hard wooden bench of a carter's wagon, had continued with a three-day trip inside a crowded stagecoach, then finally concluded with a six-hour ride down the canal.

As luck would have it, there were ninety-seven passengers aboard the canal boat, and ninety-six of them were sheep. Though Marianne had been obliged to hold a handkerchief over her nose for the entire trip, she had not minded the hardship or the discomfort. She could think of nothing but her imminent arrival at her new home.

Bibb Grange. What a beautiful name. No music ever written sounded sweeter to her ears. And it was all hers. Hers! And she dared anyone to try to take it from her.

Her great-aunt Gertrude had attempted to do so. "There is, of course, only one acceptable thing a young lady in your position can do," Gertrude Posner had said once she had finished reading the letter aloud. "You must put the entire matter in my solicitor's hands and let him sell the place for you."

*Sell it!* Marianne had bitten her bottom lip to stop the angry words that threatened to explode from her mouth.

"Once the property is sold," Aunt Gertrude had continued, "my solicitor can invest the proceeds for you to ensure you a comfortable old age. You will, of course, remain here as my companion. Any other course of action would be unacceptable."

*Remain here? Not if Hades should freeze over!*

As if the words had been spoken, Gertrude Posner pushed the pince-nez spectacles back up on her thin, sharp nose, the better to glare at her great-niece. "For a young lady in your position, Marianne, there is no other option."

"But there is, Aunt."

Marianne lifted her hand to her neck so she might touch the watch fob that had belonged her mother. Daisy McCord had worn the golden acorn on a chain, never taking it off, and Marianne liked to think that some of her mother's spirit still clung to the precious metal and the pretty green stone locked forever inside the gold filigree.

Marianne wrapped her fingers around the fob, praying it would give her the strength needed to withstand her aunt's arguments. "The house and property are mine," she said. "The letter stated that fact quite clearly. Why a gentleman I never even heard of should bequeath his estate to my mother, I cannot even guess. And frankly, I do not care what his reasons were. All I know is that I have a home of my own at last, and I have every intention of taking up residence there."

Gertrude Posner gasped. "Pure folly! A gel, alone? Why, 'tis scandalous. Before the first sunset, your reputation would be in tatters."

"Nevertheless, I am going to Derbyshire."

"You cannot mean it."

"But I do. With every ounce of resolve in me, I mean it. In my entire life I have never meant anything so much. The letter said I was to receive two hundred pounds per annum and that I could draw upon the account for up to fifty pounds each quarter day. I shall go to the bank first thing tomorrow; then, as soon as travel arrangements can be made, I shall leave for Chelmford."

"Foolish, headstrong gel. You cannot go. I . . . I forbid it!"

"Even so, Aunt, I am for Chelmford."

"You would ignore my wishes in this matter?" Not waiting for a reply, her great-aunt wadded the letter into a ball and tossed it toward the fire. "Rude, ungrateful gel! Was it not *I* who fed and clothed you these past nine years?"

"It was, Aunt, and I—"

"I took you in when your own grandfather would have nothing to do with you. You, a penniless orphan with little to recommend you. No beauty to speak of. No accomplishments. No skills with which to make yourself truly useful. Why, without my charity, you would have been destitute, without food to eat or a roof over your head!"

Marianne rose from the slipper chair in which she sat and walked over to the fireplace. Bending down, she retrieved the letter her aunt had not even let her read for herself, then she pressed the vellum smooth again. "Honesty compels me to admit that I owe you much, Aunt, even as I have acknowledged it hundreds of times these past nine years. Still, I am going to Derbyshire."

There had been many such battles of will during the two weeks that followed, but Marianne had remained adamant. And now, here she was.

After assuring herself that her reticule still contained the solicitor's letter, the deed of ownership, and the thirty pounds that remained after paying for her trip, Marianne prepared to leave the boat. She touched the golden acorn that was on a chain around her neck, hoping it would bring her luck, then she descended the gangplank and stepped onto the dock, her journey finally at an end.

As it turned out, her journey needed another two hours. After walking up the steep towpath that led to the village, one of the canalmen trailing behind her, her trunk hoisted on his shoulder, she had discovered that Chelmford was another village entirely.

"This be Matlock," the innkeeper at the Dog and Bear informed her, his accent sounding soft and rather musical after the flatter speech she had become accustomed to hearing. "Unless you're ter be met, miss, you'll be wanting ter hire a gig or sommit ter take you on ter Chelmford. Sixteen miles from here it be."

"I am not being met," she replied.

To her surprise, the innkeeper leaned forward, lowering his voice as he spoke. "That gentleman over there," he said, pointing toward a man who sat in a wing chair near the fire, "stopped in for a pint while the ostlers put a fresh team ter his carriage. He be traveling in a fine landau, and bound for Chelmford. Mayhap he'd take you up."

As if the tall, raven-haired man knew he was being discussed, he looked up from the newspaper he held and stared directly at Marianne. No ordinary traveler, he was dressed in what appeared to her to be the height of fashion, from his shiny black boots, with their white tops turned over just below the knees of his gray breeches, to the elegant sky-blue coat that fit his broad shoulders to perfection. He was no more than thirty or thirty-one, and though his features were rather hard-edged, and his eyes so dark a brown as to be nearly black, he was unquestionably the handsomest man Marianne had ever seen.

As for his being a gentleman, she took leave to doubt

that assumption. No *gentleman* would look at a lady the way he was doing.

Having traveled alone for the past four days, Marianne had become accustomed to brazen stares from the males she encountered. However, "brazen" did not adequately describe the way those dark eyes assessed her slender figure beneath the unfashionable straw-colored pelisse. The man took her measure from head to toe without truly noticing her face, her medium brown hair, or her gray-green eyes. He gazed at her in a knowing yet bored manner, as though he were privy to every secret held by the female sex, with no mysteries left to be solved, and his knowledgeable gaze sent a shiver of excitement up Marianne's spine.

An instant later her excitement turned to embarrassment, and she decided the man's insolent manner would set any levelheaded female's teeth on edge. Or if it did not, it should! As well, she decided she would be wiser to travel the sixteen miles to Chelmford on her knees rather than ask a favor of such a man.

She turned back to the innkeeper. "How much," she asked, her voice not quite steady, "to hire a gig and driver?"

"Four and six, miss. Will you be wanting ter rest a bit before you go? Have a cuppa tea perhaps?"

Though the thought of a cup of steaming tea made her empty stomach cry out for relief, Marianne shook her head. She wanted to put distance between her and the man beside the fire. "I should like to start immediately, if that is possible. I am not perfectly sure of my destination, and I should like to reach Bibb Grange while it is still light."

When she said Bibb Grange, the man beside the fire looked up once again. He said nothing, merely stared

at her, and Marianne wondered if that handsome face
knew how to smile. Not that it was any concern of hers.
In all likelihood, once she left the inn, she would never
see the man again.

Two hours later, in need of directions, the driver of
the hired gig reined in the horse beside a sturdy arched
stone bridge constructed not more than half a century
before. The bridge, built wide enough to accommodate
carriages, spanned a pretty mill pond where graceful
white swans floated about upon the gently rippling surface.

The idyllic scene did not extend beyond the pond,
however, for to the right of the bridge stood a large
redbrick textile mill that was powered by a water wheel.
The water that spilled noisily over the wheel, turning it
at a brisk pace, flowed from a rock outcropping that
stretched farther than Marianne could see, its source
hidden by hundreds of dark green trees. Above the noise
of the water wheel she heard a muted yet steady hum
that seemed to come from inside the mill.

"What is that sound?" she asked.

"That be the looms," the driver replied. "They can
be heard night and day, six days a week. After a time,
a body gets so used to the sound, they no longer hear
it."

Marianne doubted she would ever get used to the
noise, and she prayed silently that Bibb Grange would
prove to be some distance from the village and out of
hearing of the mill and the water wheel.

The village of Chelmford, which could be seen on
the other side of the bridge and down the sloped lane
to their left, was larger than Marianne had expected,

with possibly a hundred cottages visible and perhaps twenty shops and an inn. All the cottages and shops were of a similar size and built of a similar grayish limestone, and, paradoxically, the sameness of the structures made the village unlike any Marianne had ever seen before.

At one time Chelmford must have been a neat, tidy village, though now several of the cottages looked deserted, while others showed definite signs of neglect. Shutters sagged on broken hinges, windowpanes went missing entirely, and numerous roofs were in need of rethatching.

"What sort of place is this?" she asked.

" 'Twere built as a model village," the driver said. "My pap lived here as a lad, and his pap worked in the mill. A weaver, he was."

As if more than willing to talk, he pointed northward, where the top of an erratic crenellated roof and a tower could be seen, their silvery limestone appearing dramatically pale against the brilliant green of a thinly wooded slope. "The old viscount, him as was grandfer to the present one, lived up there, and when he inherited, he built the textile mill and the village to give the folks at Chelmford work outside the mines."

Marianne knew little of mills. Having lived in Wales, however, she knew more than she wanted to about mines—and about the wretched conditions under which the miners worked. She'd seen children no more than four or five years old walking through the streets, their faces covered with the black dust of the mines and their thin bodies stooped from hours on their hands and knees, pulling carts through the shallow tunnels belowground.

"Used water power for the mill," the driver continued.

"Everything of the finest, or so my pap said. Modern equipment. Even set up a school for the young'uns, the old viscount did. Wouldn't employ none under twelve years old, and he popped in at the mill and the school every so often, unexpected like, to make sure things was run the way he wanted."

"Good for the viscount."

"Folks come from all over wanting to be taken on at the mill. Nearly eight hundred there were at one time, with the mill going day and night. My pap says the place were something like back then."

"What happened?"

The driver shrugged his thin shoulders. "The old viscount died and the new one inherited. Spent all his time in London, the sixth viscount did, seldom even came to Derbyshire for a visit. Now he's gone and his son's the newest viscount. Most of the folks here about never even clamped eyes on viscount number seven." The driver said no more, as if the absence of two generations of owners explained in full the fate of the mill and the village.

"Ho, lad," he called to a passing youngster, "you know a place called Bibb Grange?"

"That way," the boy said, pointing up the same lane that gave access to the estate of the owner of the mill and the village. "Follow the lane ter the first break in the wall. Turn left. You'll see the grange right enough."

After thanking the lad, the driver followed the lane for two miles, until he came to a break in the low drystone wall where an iron gate had once stood. The gate lay on the ground several feet away, rusted and forsaken, with dark-pink ragged robin poking their heads up through the once-lovely bars.

The driver deftly guided the horse though the opening, and as the shod hooves *clop-clopped* on the hard-packed earth of the carriageway, Marianne closed her eyes and held her breath, praying that the fallen gate was not an omen of things to come.

"Like the lad said, miss, there it be, right enough."

Marianne opened her eyes and breathed a sigh of relief. Like the short carriageway, the house was not grand. It contained no more than ten or twelve rooms, but there was a story above the first level as well as an attic with dormer windows. The exterior of the house was fashioned of redbrick, with medieval stone the same silvery gray as the viscount's rambling abode forming a shallow arch over the entrance. The steeply slanted roof was thatched, and at least as far as Marianne could see, each of the mullioned windows was intact.

Three shallow steps gave access to an unpretentious entrance door whose thick oak was dark with age, and while the driver unstrapped Marianne's trunk from the back of the gig, the new owner climbed the steps and lifted the knocker. Within a matter of seconds, the door was swung open.

"Yes?" inquired a middle-aged woman. "What be you wanting?"

Since the woman wore neither apron nor cap, Marianne could not be certain she was a servant. And yet, her gray hair was pulled back in a thick, unfashionable bun, and her dress was made of rough but serviceable linsey-woolsey, topped with a freshly starched fichu.

"Is this Bibb Grange?" Marianne asked.

"It be that, but the owner bin dead these six months, and there be no one at home ter receive visitors."

The woman stepped back, her obvious intention to close the oak door, so Marianne spoke up rather quickly.

"I am not a visitor. I am Miss Marianne McCord, the new owner."

The woman's eyes widened in disbelief, then she peeped around Marianne as if looking for a carriage and servants.

Reminded of what her great-aunt had said about the neighborhood being scandalized by the arrival of a single, unchaperoned female, Marianne lifted her chin, the gesture as defiant as she could make it. "As you see, I am alone. I have neither abigail nor chaperone, nor will I have either of those persons in the future. I am, however, the owner of Bibb Grange, with the deed to prove it, and whoever you may be, I wish you will stand aside so that I may enter my new home."

After bobbing a begrudging curtsy, the woman stepped aside and Marianne entered the vestibule. At first the interior appeared rather shabby, for the carpet was sadly worn around the edges, and the console table against the right wall was an inch thick in dust. Upon closer inspection, however, Marianne noticed a lovely old staircase, its wooden balustrade composed of charmingly carved panels depicting mythical and woodland creatures. As if in complement to the staircase, the creamy white plaster ceiling was decorated with garlands of crisp leaves. "Oh," she said, "how lovely."

"The roof leaks," the woman muttered, "and there be not a clean-drawing chimney in the house. As for the mice that invade the larder—"

"Excuse me," Marianne said, not at all happy to be bombarded with the shortcomings of the house in her first minute of residence, "but you have not told me who you are."

"Mrs. Fannon," she replied. "Housekeeper to old Mr. Bibb for twenty years."

"Are you alone here?"

"Of course not. There be Mr. Fannon and Cook. The two maids and the groom were let go as soon as old Mr. Bibb took sick. No point in having three extra mouths to feed when there's little work to be done."

Marianne let her gaze slide to the dusty console table, but she kept her comments to herself. Enough time for that tomorrow. For now, the driver had brought her trunk and set it inside the vestibule.

"Will that be all, miss?"

While Marianne searched in her reticule, then handed the driver a suitable vail, Mrs. Fannon said, "If you want the trunk abovestairs, best have the driver take it up for you. There be no one about for such tasks."

"What of your husband?"

"Fannon be coachman. He don't work inside the house."

Suffering from both fatigue and hunger, Marianne felt her temper rising due to the housekeeper's insolent manner. Accustomed to biting her tongue, however, she strove to keep her anger in check. "Please show the driver where to take the trunk."

"The master bedchamber b'aint usable. It be just as it was when old Mr. Bibb died."

The thought crossed Marianne's mind that the sheets might not have been changed on the master bed, and after suppressing a shudder at the morbid image that conjured, she instructed the housekeeper to direct the driver to whichever of the rooms was cleanest. "Then open the windows, if you please, and see to airing the bedding. I shall await you in"—she pointed to a door to the right—"in there. Once you have seen to the bedchamber, I should like a light repast. It need not be anything fancy, tea and toast will suffice. After I have eaten, I shall expect to be shown to my room."

Marianne slept quite late the next morning, though how she had ever managed to fall asleep was a mystery. The housekeeper had led her to a musty, cell-like room abovestairs, a room whose mattress felt as though it had been stuffed with chestnut hulls. As luck would have it, once Marianne had found the only comfortable spot in the disreputable bedding, a rodent had begun to gnaw inside the wall behind the headboard of the bed. The incessant *chomp-chomp-chomp* had kept her awake for hours, nearly driving her insane.

And yet, she had finally slept, and now she arose feeling surprisingly refreshed and eager to get to work setting her house in order. But the work could wait until she had broken her fast—broken it with a sizable meal! At least half a roasted ox came to mind, with side dishes of eggs and fruit, accompanied by fresh baked bread.

The thought of consuming such a repast spurred her to hurry her ablutions, after which she rummaged through her trunk for her oldest dress and a coverall apron. Suitably attired to set herself and the three servants to the task of scrubbing Bibb Grange from ground floor to attic, Marianne descended the staircase that had charmed her the day before, running her hand along the wooden panels to touch first a carved bird on the wing, then a doe and a fawn who drank at a stream.

Wrinkling her nose in distaste at the dust that adhered to her fingertips, Marianne strode purposefully toward the kitchen at the rear of the house, her boots echoing loudly on the wide plank floor of the short corridor. Only when she opened the kitchen door did it occur to her that the house was surprisingly quiet. As well it should have been, for the place was deserted. No welcoming fire burned in the wide stone fireplace, nor was there any sign that a morning meal had been prepared or eaten.

Upon the wide deal table, a single sheet of cheap notepaper had been left, kept in place by a thick crockery mug. Marianne retrieved the paper and read the few brief lines scribbled in pencil. There was no opening salutation; there was no complimentary close; there was only the terse message.

*Thirty years I've been in service, but never have I served in any but a gentleman's establishment. Nor will I start now. Fannon and I have packed our belongings and left. Cook too.*

Though she assumed the note had been written by the housekeeper, the voice inside Marianne's head was that of her great-aunt. Had Gertrude Posner been correct? Would no respectable servants work for an unchaperoned single woman? Would they judge her without knowing anything more of her than those two facts?

For a full minute Marianne stood in the middle of the kitchen, her mind a blank, unable to think what was best to do. Thankfully, that indecision fled almost as quickly as it had come, replaced by a determination that straightened her back and caused her chin to jut in a decidedly stubborn manner. Life had never treated Marianne McCord with velvet gloves, and apparently it meant to go on as it had begun.

"So be it!" she said. "I have lived most of my life without the approval of those around me. Furthermore,

I have cooked and cleaned and lived to tell the tale. If I must do so again, at least it will be in my own home, on my own land."

When her mother had become ill and Marianne had been obliged to choose between purchasing the needed medicines and paying for the services of a maid of all work, the choice had been clear. For the final year of Daisy McCord's life, her daughter had been nurse, cook, maid, and friend, and she had never regretted a day of it.

Only when the seventeen-year-old Marianne was sent to her great-aunt were servants again a part of her experience. At that time, of course, the grieving girl had cared little where she lived or under what circumstances. It was only later that she realized there was a price to be paid for the easy life.

For the privilege of living with her great-aunt and being waited upon by servants, Marianne had been obliged to give up total freedom of thought and action, never daring to contradict the decrees of her zealously moral relative. All the while, her every move was watched and judged, as though her aunt waited for that moment when Marianne would finally disgrace herself.

Reminding herself that she had put all that behind her, Marianne strode over to the larder in search of food. Unfortunately, the Fannons must have rewarded themselves with whatever edibles the house contained, for the shelves in the smallish pantry held nothing but a wedge of cheese that bore suspicious tooth marks, and the heel of a loaf of bread. Since the larder proved no cleaner than the front portion of the house, Marianne turned her back on the unpalatable-looking food.

She had meant to spend the day putting her house in order, but it appeared she would be obliged to go to the village first thing. Either that or starve. Since her stomach had been making growling noises this hour and more, she rethought her priorities. Before any other project was undertaken, she must purchase food and find a capable mouser. No. *Two* mousers!

After returning to the small bedchamber to don a pale green dress, a darker green spencer, and a small-poked straw bonnet suitable to wear to the village, it occurred to Marianne to have a look-in at the stable she had seen from the window of her tiny room. Five minutes later, a basket over her arm, she did just that, and all things considered, the stable turned out to be a pleasant surprise. The six-stall building smelled of fresh-strewn hay, and the stone floor had been scrubbed recently, making it noticeably cleaner than the floor of the kitchen.

To the new owner's delight, she discovered within the limestone walls an ancient trap and an equally ancient dappled gray mare. The black leather of the trap's divided seat was cracked in several places, obliging a hopeful passenger to choose her position carefully, and the aged mare was swaybacked and presumably deaf. Still, the trap rolled and the mare walked, so all in all, Marianne considered herself a fortunate woman.

Though a competent rider, she had never handled the ribbons before, and after harnessing the mare to the trap, she climbed aboard with some trepidation. As it turned out, she need not have worried about her lack of skill, for the mare needed no controlling. The animal had only one pace, and that one so sluggish it was little better than a crawl, but the mare pulled the trap down the carriageway without complaint, then turned right onto the lane, obviously well acquainted with the route to Chelmford.

While the placid equine plodded alongside the

drystone wall, Marianne seized the opportunity to sit back, relax, and enjoy the beauty of the Derbyshire countryside. From the green, deep-cut dale on her left to the hint of wild crag miles away to her right, she found it all splendid, though she did wonder where the peaks were in this Peak District.

Accustomed to Wales, where there was an excess of rainfall, Marianne found the dry lane smooth traveling, with sunshine filtering through the leaves of the birch and oak trees, dappling the hard-packed earth. In time the newcomer became lost in quiet contemplation, her senses lulled by the soft *clop-clop* of the mare's hooves and the gentle, pleasing song of a dunnock perched on a low limb.

For some reason, the little bird suddenly took wing, and gradually Marianne was drawn from her reverie by the sound of galloping hooves. At first the sound was rather faint, but as it grew louder, becoming a steady pounding, she began to feel uneasy. She looked over first one shoulder, then the other, and had only just determined that the source of the noise was to her right, and coming closer by the minute, when she spied a rider astride a powerful looking black horse. To her dismay, horse and rider were galloping toward her at a dangerous speed.

The animal was at least sixteen hands high, with a straight back and strong, well-muscled neck and shoulders, and at the moment those muscles were bunched to jump the low stone wall. Unfortunately, Marianne was on the other side of that wall, in the direct path of the potentially lethal horse, and she knew all too well what might happen if those steel-shod hooves connected with her head.

Even if she had known how to get herself and the

trap out of harm's way, the mare would not have responded, for the animal, oblivious of the impending danger, merely continued in her same lumbering manner. Marianne, feeling as helpless as a fox caught in a snare, watched the black's powerful hooves lift off the ground, and with no other choice left to her, she screamed and threw herself from the leather seat, landing facedown in the grayish dust of the lane.

# Two

While Marianne curled herself into as small a ball as possible, her knees pulled up to her chest and her arms drawn protectively over her head, she felt rather than saw the horse and rider sail over the wall, completely missing the trap and the still-placid mare.

"Damnation!" the rider shouted.

Marianne heard the man's curse, then she heard a high-pitched animal squeal followed by a thud, as though someone had landed hard upon the ground. As she lay there in the lane, her breathing coming in gasps and the pounding of her heart clamoring in her ears, she heard a neigh of distress. There was no other sound—no cursing, no threats of reprisal from the rider—only the frightened neighing of the horse.

Rising cautiously, Marianne spied the black standing unattended not more than ten feet away from her, his reins hanging free and dragging the ground. He bobbed his massive head up and down, his black silk mane flying with the movement while his eyes rolled in fear and confusion. Slowly, hesitantly, he took first one exploratory step, then another, all the while favoring his off-rear leg. As for the rider, that gentleman lay unmoving upon the ground, apparently pitched from the saddle.

Marianne could not attend to both man and beast,

and since the horse was closest to her, she went to him first, moving slowly and crooning soothing nonsense all the while, until she was able to catch his bridle. After stroking the animal's forelock and breathing softly into his nostrils, she was able to calm him enough that he allowed her to walk him over to a nearby birch tree, where she tied his reins to a low-hanging limb. Giving him a cursory examination, she found that he had grazed the cannon bone of his off-rear leg. Thankfully, his injury was not life threatening.

Once the horse was secured, Marianne went to the rider, who lay unmoving. His hat was nowhere to be seen, and his face was turned away from her so that she saw only his thick, dark hair. "Sir," she said, touching the man's shoulder. "Are you all right? May I be of help?"

The man groaned, then he turned his head to look at her. If the anger that flashed in his dark eyes was anything to judge by, he did not appreciate her offer of help. "Idiot!" he said, his breath labored. "Have you no more sense than to ride into the path of an oncoming horse?"

It was Marianne's turn to groan, for the rider was none other than the man she had seen in the inn the previous day, and he was far from happy to see her again. With his mouth set in an angry straight line, he muttered, "Who let you abroad without a keeper?"

Still shaken by the accident, and in no mood to be yelled at, Marianne spoke more sharply than she intended. "I might ask you why you did not look where you were going? And while I am asking, I should like to know who gave you permission to gallop across my land as though pursued by the furies."

"Your land?"

"Yes. This land belongs to Bibb Grange, and—"

"Madam, we shall argue boundaries at some later date. For the moment, I should like to know the status of my horse. Is he badly injured?"

"He has a grazed cannon. Otherwise, I believe him to be unharmed."

"You are certain?"

"As certain as I can be."

When he said nothing more, she asked, "What of you? Are you injured?"

"Merely winded, no thanks to you."

The man sat up, though he moved slowly, his hand pressed to his right side.

"If you lean on me, sir, perhaps I can assist you to stand."

The coldness in those eyes told Marianne he would like to refuse her assistance, but he must have thought better of that option, for without further comment he placed his arm around her shoulders. Though she had never been this close to a man before, had never felt a strong male arm around her, she maintained her composure and helped him to his feet. When his blue-gray coat fell open, however, she forgot all about his muscular arm, for she saw red smudges staining the silver stripes of his white waistcoat. To her horror, the smudges appeared to be growing wider.

"Oh! Sir, you are more than winded. You are injured, for you are bleeding from your side."

" 'Tis an old wound," he said, his words clipped, as though spoken through pain.

"But it bleeds as if fresh."

"If you must know, I took part in a duel a few days ago, at which time I was shot."

"A duel! But they are illegal."

Marianne swallowed the many questions that sprang to her mind. As well, she kept to herself her opinion of a person who would be so foolish as to ride a spirited horse only days after sustaining a gunshot wound.

As if the rider read her thoughts, he said, "I believed the wound to be healed."

"You were mistaken. And now it wants attention." Considering the state of the grange, Marianne felt certain she would not find anything there suitable for binding such a wound. "Unfortunately, sir, I cannot offer you the hospitality of my house. Therefore, I suggest you allow me to help you into the trap, so that I may drive you to your home."

"Very well," he said, the resignation in his tone implying his wish for an alternate plan. Still, he allowed her to help him into the divided seat.

Once Marianne had tied the injured black to the rear of the trap and climbed aboard, her back to the gentleman's back, she asked, "Where to, sir?"

"Up there," he said, pointing toward the crenellated roof. "About a mile up the lane."

Surprised, Marianne spoke before she thought. "Are you the new viscount?"

"I am," he replied, his face stony and forbidding. "But before you get any ideas, young woman, allow me to inform you that I am in Derbyshire on a repairing lease. I have no wish to be neighborly."

"How fortunate that you told me," she said, embarrassed by his rudeness and his assumption that she would try to foist herself upon him in the future. "I would not have guessed it otherwise, yours being such a *friendly* nature."

As if taken aback by her audacity, he turned to stare at her, his face mere inches from hers. Finally, the corners of his mouth twitched the least little bit, as if he tried to suppress a smile. "I suppose you think I should apologize for my temper."

"I was thinking nothing of the sort, my lord. I was too busy wondering how it came about that a man with your charming disposition possessed only *one* bullet hole in his person."

This time he did smile. "Madam, you have the manners of a fishwife."

"And, you, sir, have no manners at all."

"I know," he said. "It is my most endearing quality."

Marianne felt her own lips twitch, but she said no more, merely lifted the ribbons and made a clicking noise to the mare, turning the animal so they traveled back up the lane. Considering the injured gelding tied behind the trap, and the man who sat on the other side of the divided seat, bloodstaining the side of his waist-coat, Marianne was happy the mare moved at such a slow pace.

Twenty minutes were needed to travel the upward-sloping mile from the scene of the accident to the gate-house at Jenson Hall, then an additional ten minutes were required to traverse the winding carriageway to the house itself. As a result of that half hour spent in prox-imity, their shoulders often touching when the wheels of the trap hit an uneven spot in the lane, the two ad-joining landowners came to an unspoken truce.

Their silence was broken by Marianne's gasp upon first seeing the entire Hall. "Oh, my," she said.

It was an impressive edifice, ranged around a central court with an extensive wing to the right, the rectangu-lar tower to the left, and a smaller building beside the tower that Marianne thought must be a chapel. The tower, so the viscount told her, was twelfth century, while the wing was quite new. "Built not more than two hundred years ago."

"Very impressive."

"What of the grange?" he asked. "I am practically a newcomer here, so I know little of its history."

"Nor do I. The dust on the furniture might well be from a previous century, but I believe the house is of a more recent date."

The viscount chuckled. "And are you pleased with your new property? Does it meet your expectations and your requirements."

"I had no idea what to expect. As for my requirements, I need only a roof over my head and an opportunity to make the grange my home. Oh," she added with a grimace, "and a couple of good mousers."

"Mousers?"

"Yes." She waved her hand toward the Hall. "Do you suppose there is within that magnificent crenellated pile of rock such a thing as a spare cat, or one with kittens?"

"I have no idea. This is only the second time I have ever visited the place, and the first time was at least a dozen years ago. However, I shall be happy to ask after such an animal."

When they stopped at the entrance, which consisted of a rather anticlimactic wooden door with a simple two-foot overhang, a very proper butler and a liveried footman appeared on the instant. Marianne could not help noticing the difference between the viscount's reception at the Hall and her own at the grange. As for the servants, there was no comparison between his minions and hers—or, more properly, her former servants.

The viscount's house, though without its owner for years, appeared as clean and habitable as though he lived there all year round, and his servants, though practically strangers to him, hurried forward to see to his needs.

"My lord," the butler said, concern on his wrinkled face, "are you injured, sir? Shall I send for the apothecary?"

"No. My man can do what is needed. Just help me down, Sykes, and have one of the stable lads see to Mercury. According to this young lady, who was kind enough to bring me home, the gelding has a grazed cannon."

"Right away, my lord."

While the footman untied the gelding and began leading him at a slow pace toward the stable, the butler gave the viscount a hand to the ground. When they were on a level, the servant asked in a hushed voice, "Shall I send for Mrs. King, my lord?"

"Why the devil should I want the housekeeper?"

The butler cleared his throat and glanced toward Marianne. "The young lady, my lord. I thought perhaps a cup of tea."

Marianne felt her face grow warm. "Oh, no. I thank you, but I am bound for the village."

She could not help but notice that the viscount breathed a sigh of relief when she refused the invitation, and recalling his earlier remark that he had no wish to be neighborly, she lifted the reins and clicked to the mare. Fortunately, the mare had two paces—full stop and moving—so once the animal obeyed the directive to turn around, it continued down the carriageway without waiting for further instruction.

To Marianne's surprise, the viscount called after her. "Thank you, Miss . . ."

"Marianne McCord," she replied.

After a wave of her hand, Marianne gave her attention

to the mare and never once looked back at the tall, handsome man who had not bothered to introduce himself. Not that it mattered that he had not done so. By his own admission, the viscount was in Chelmford on a repairing lease, and once he was well again, he would probably return to London or to one of his other estates. In all likelihood, Marianne would never have an occasion to use his name.

When she finally reached the village, Marianne let the mare guide her to the proper shops. After crossing the stone bridge that spanned the pond and plodding past the noisy water wheel and the equally noisy redbrick textile mill, the animal stopped at a small shop in whose open window hung a lamb shank and a plucked goose. Above the door was displayed a hand-lettered sign reading WETHINGTON'S, and as Marianne climbed down from the trap, a youth of about fourteen came out to catch the reins of the mare.

The youth, whose hair bore an unfortunate resemblance to a haystack, had yet to grow into his overlong arms and legs, but he patted the mare's withers in a gentle, caring manner that gained him a whicker of greeting from the swaybacked animal. " 'Ello, Bess," he said. " 'Ow are you, old girl?"

Happy to know the animal's name, Marianne smiled at the lad. "Bess has had rather a busy afternoon. Could you give her a drink while I make my purchases?"

Though the youth gave her a questioning look, as if wondering why a stranger was driving Bess, and why that stranger was liberally covered with dust, he touched his forelock politely. "Yes, miss."

Because the day was sunny and mild, the shop door

stood open. After shaking the dust from her skirt and straightening her bonnet, Marianne crossed the threshold of the shop, discovering a larger establishment than expected. The shelves that lined the side and rear walls, though neat and well displayed, held only half as much foodstuffs and merchandise as they might have, and she was reminded that the village was not as prosperous as it had once been.

"May I help you?" asked a thin, balding man in his fifties.

"I will wait my turn," Marianne replied, indicating one of the villagers who stood beside the thread shelf. The customer, a pretty red-haired woman of perhaps thirty, held a spool of blue thread against a square of inexpensive blue linsey-woolsey, obviously trying to decide if the two shades matched.

"Hannah b'aint in no hurry," the man said. Since he wore an apron over his waistcoat and breeches, Marianne assumed he was the shopkeeper. "Are you Mr. Wethington?"

"I am," he replied, his tone wary.

Not surprised at a villager's distrust of a stranger, Marianne told herself not to take offense. "How do you do?" she said, donning her friendliest smile. "I am Miss McCord, the new owner of Bibb Grange, and I have come straightaway to restock the grange larder." She placed her list of necessities upon the worn deal counter, pushing the paper toward him. "I shall need a number of items, and have made a list of—"

"Mrs. Fannon buys for t'grange," he said.

As if that were an end to the matter, the shopkeeper did not even bother to read Marianne's list; instead, he pulled a cloth from beneath the counter and began to dust the shelf directly behind him. Employing real enthusiasm to the task, he rearranged three or four of the colored bottles of elixirs and pills, moving them just so until they were in perfect alignment.

Though taken aback by the apparent snub, Marianne managed to maintain a semblance of civility by taking a deep breath and letting it out slowly. It was a trick she had learned soon after going to live with her great-aunt, when she discovered that Gertrude Posner tolerated no opinion that differed from her own.

"As you will probably discover soon enough," Marianne said, "Mrs. Fannon and her husband have chosen to leave the grange."

"Already know that," Wethington replied, attacking another shelf with his dusting cloth. "Cook too, I hear."

"Yes, the cook as well. For that reason, I shall be purchasing the supplies for the grange. At least until such time as I find suitable replacements for the previous servants."

"Won't find no replacements, *Miss* McCord. Leastways, not here in Chelmford."

Marianne had just about reached her limit for tolerating rudeness from strangers, and she was obliged to bite her bottom lip to keep from giving voice to a word she learned in her youth from a stable lad. Her stomach was rumbling with hunger, she had a filthy house awaiting her attention, and all she wanted was some provisions so she might return to that house and set to work making it habitable.

After taking another deep breath, she said, "When you have filled my list, Mr. Wethington, you will find me waiting outside."

She had only just turned to retrace her steps to the door, when the shopkeeper spoke again. "Cash only," he said.

Marianne gasped, as did the red-haired woman beside the thread shelf. Here was insult indeed, for only the village drunk and certain types of females were denied the convenience of an account. Aware of the significance of the request for cash, Marianne felt her face burning with the combined heat of embarrassment and anger.

Anger won out, and after reaching inside her reticule and producing two pound notes, she returned to the counter and slapped the money down upon the worn wood. "This should cover the expenses," she said. "But be warned, Mr. Wethington, I expect the best your shop has to offer. Should I receive anything less, I will not hesitate to visit the Hall, where I shall speak with my neighbor, the viscount. He is, I believe, the owner of both the village and this shop."

At the mention of the viscount, the shopkeeper wheeled around, dropping his cloth. If he expected to see the new owner of Bibb Grange, however, he was disappointed, for she had exited the shop, slamming the door in her wake.

To give herself time to achieve a degree of serenity, Marianne did not wait beside the mare but walked down the street, past a few shops and the inn, with its swan-shaped sign above the door. Her brisk pace was exceeded only by her fast-turning brain. Unfortunately, any hope that the walk might restore her usually pleasant disposition was dashed by the reception she received at the blacksmith's shop.

Having spied a likely-looking tabby grooming its hind leg in the sunshine just outside the smithy's, and recalling the fallen entrance gate at the grange, Marianne stepped just inside the open door and spoke to the rather surly-looking fellow wielding a bellows.

"Good afternoon," she said. "I saw your cat outside,

and I wondered if you knew where I might find a good
mouser."

"B'aint no extra cats about," he replied, his tone
matching his looks.

Not completely put off, Marianne asked about having
the wrought iron gate rehung. "I should imagine it will
require new linchpins."

The smithy swiped a faded bandanna across his face
to remove the sweat caused by the increased heat of the
fire in the forge. "I be too busy just now, missus."

"It need not be seen to today. What of tomorrow or
the next day? Or even one day next week?"

"Busy then too."

Not being one of those people who need a wall to
fall upon them, Marianne said, "And next month? I suppose you will be too busy then as well."

"Don't know when I'd be able ter get around ter any
repairs at t'grange."

Having said his piece, the smith picked up a long,
heavy tong and removed a still-burning horseshoe from
the fire in the forge. Turning his back to Marianne, he
dunked the horseshoe into a barrel of water, where the
hot metal sizzled and sent steam into the air. He remained thus even after the sizzling had stopped, his
back to Marianne, leaving her in no doubt that word of
her unmarried status had reached the entire village.

There was no door to slam at the blacksmith's, but
Marianne exited the place with her head held high.
Thankfully, when she reached Wethington's once again,
the lad with the haystack hair was loading the final
package onto the seat of the trap.

"Here, miss," he said, his hand outstretched, "this be
your change."

Marianne took the coins and dropped them into her

reticule. "Thank you," she said. "I am happy to know there is at least one person in Chelmford who—"

She stopped abruptly, for the lad had touched his finger to his forelock, then had turned and hurried back inside the shop.

Still fuming with anger at the all-too-familiar narrowmindedness of the villagers, Marianne tried, but without success, to hurry the mare across the bridge. Bess would not be hurried, of course, so it was several minutes before they had finally left the mill and the water wheel behind. The noise of the falling water was still a faint hum in the background when Marianne spied someone standing in the middle of the lane, her hand raised as if she wished Marianne to stop.

Upon recognizing the red-haired woman who had been choosing a spool of thread in Wethington's shop, Marianne reined in the mare. The moment they stopped, the woman approached the trap and dropped a curtsy. "Afternoon, miss."

Not at all certain she wished to encounter another one of the villagers, Marianne merely nodded.

For some reason, the woman chose to ignore Marianne's rudeness. "My name is Hannah Scott," she said, "and I couldn't help hearing your conversation with Mr. Wethington."

Marianne felt her face grow warm, knowing that someone had been witness to the snub. If the woman noticed the blush, however, she gave no indication of it. She appeared far too concerned with what she wished to say. "I . . . I heard what you said about the Fannons and the cook leaving the grange, miss, and about you needing a suitable replacement, and I—"

"You wished to add your opinion to that of the shop-keeper," Marianne said, her words clipped with anger. "Well, Hannah Scott, you need not have bothered, for I perfectly understand the situation. The shopkeeper said no one would work for me, and it is apparent that he was in the right of it, for the blacksmith as good as refused to fix my gate."

"I'll do it."

Marianne blinked, unsure what the woman meant by the terse remark. "You will do what?"

"I'll work for you. I know how to keep house, and I'm a fair cook, if I do say so as shouldn't. I'm a good needlewoman, and I'm careful not to scorch what I iron." She paused only long enough to take a breath. "I'll even try my hand at that gate you mentioned, though I can't make any promises there."

Too astonished to speak, Marianne merely stared at the woman.

"You won't have to pay me the same wages as old Mr. Bibb gave Mrs. Fannon, me not being a real house-keeper, and all. Fact is, I don't need much. Just a roof over my head and a little money to put by for my old age."

"It is not the money, I assure you. I was merely taken by surprise at your catalogue of qualifications."

"If you're worried I'm not a good worker, just ask anyone. They'll tell you Hannah Scott is not afeared of hard work. Been doing it all my life. And if you can see your way clear to hiring me, miss, I'll make sure you never have cause to regret it."

The last of her naivety left back in the village, Marianne looked long and hard at the woman in the road. Hannah Scott was a handsome woman with the blue eyes and rose-and-cream complexion that usually accompany red hair, and though she was much too young to be a housekeeper, the expression in those blue eyes seemed sincere. And yet, Marianne felt instinctively that some important ingredient had been left out of the woman's story.

"You would be willing to work for me for less money than Mrs. Fannon earned?"

"Yes, ma'am."

"Why is that, I wonder?"

When the woman said nothing, Marianne continued. "I should also like to know why you would be willing to be in the employ of someone whose circumstances appear to be a thorn in the village's moral side?"

"I can't be worrying about the villagers, miss. I got me and my boy to think of." She looked down at her hands, the fingers laced together as if to keep them from revealing that she was far from calm. "I got a son. He's twelve years old, but he's small for his age and has a shy way about him. I need to get him away from the village, where there's a pair of bullies who won't leave him in peace."

"I see. And what of the boy's father?"

Like many people who possess red hair, when Hannah Scott blushed, she blushed all over. Her face, her neck, even the lobes of her ears, showed color. "B'aint married," she said, the words spoken defiantly. "Never have been. If that offends you, ma'am, you've only to say so, and I'll be on my way."

As if needing to feel the strength of her mother's spirit, Marianne touched the golden filigree fob at her neck. "I am not offended," she said quietly.

Hannah Scott breathed a sigh of relief. "The boy and me live with my papa. We always have. Papa's a good man, truly he is, for he never once threatened to throw me out, even when I refused to tell him the name of the gentleman who . . ." She cleared her throat. "There's plenty of fathers as wouldn't have been so forgiving. Still, me and Georgie shame Papa. Though he never says so, I believe he would be happier if me and my boy weren't there, all the time reminding him and the neighbors of what I . . ."

Though Hannah's words trailed away, Marianne had no trouble filling in the remainder of the sentence. No trouble at all. She was well acquainted with the ways of shamed relatives, just as she was no stranger to the slights of sanctimonious neighbors. Fortunately, as a female child she had been spared the threats of bullies. Still, whispers and snubs had been all too familiar occurrences in her young life.

"When can you start?" she asked.

"Oh, miss," Hannah Scott said, bobbing another curtsy. "Is tomorrow too soon?"

Remembering the deplorable state of her newly acquired home, Marianne said, "This instant would not be too soon. However, I imagine you have arrangements to make, so I will not ask you to rush them."

"You don't need to ask, miss. Me and Georgie—that's my boy, Georgie—will be up to the grange before nightfall."

Though Marianne attempted to stop the trap near the weed-choked kitchen garden, her hope to unload her supplies more conveniently, the mare had other plans. The single-minded beast ignored both bribery and threats, and blithely disregarded an ill-spoken word or two—words no lady should know, never mind say. Instead, Bess merely continued her slow pace all the way to the stable, not pausing until her metal shoes *clink-clinked* upon the stone floor.

Frustrated, Marianne muttered a few well-chosen epithets at the ancient mare, then she climbed down from the trap and walked around to the other side to see to the packages, letting the animal stand where she had stopped. "If you think I will reward such recalcitrance as you displayed with a bag of oats, you are wide of the mark."

After grabbing up an armload of supplies, Marianne spoke over her shoulder. "I will see to you later, you stubborn old nab girder!"

Having said her piece, she turned toward the house. It was only when she emerged from the shaded dimness of the stable into the late afternoon sunshine that she discovered she had a visitor.

"Lord Jenson!"

"Miss McCord," the viscount said, his eyebrow lifted in a totally spurious display of shock. "I claim acquaintance with a number of accomplished young ladies, but there can be no doubt that you take the prize as the one with the most colorful vocabulary."

# Three

"Sir! You startled me."

A smile pulled at the gentleman's well-defined lips. "No more, madam, than you startled me. Such language. Tsk, tsk."

"Gammon! I should be surprised if you had not said worse before you quit your bed this morning. And speaking of beds, why are you not in yours? Have you no consideration for your wounded side?"

"I am all patched up now, and so long as I do not attempt to leap over any more young ladies in traps, I shall most likely live to a ripe old age. Besides," he added, nodding toward a large creel that sat upon the ground, a rope tied around the lid to keep it in place, "I owed you something for delivering me to my home."

Marianne wrinkled her nose in distaste. "Fish?"

"Of course not!"

Obviously taken aback by the thought that anyone would suspect him of hauling around fish, the viscount hurried to explain that the creel happened to be the only basket with a lid. "And believe me, what I brought you needed confining. They were less than pleased to be carted about so ignominiously. As for the caterwauling, I vow, my ears are still ringing from the din."

"They? Sir, did you bring me some mousers? Oh, bless you! You cannot know how pleased I am."

From the rather breathtaking smile she bestowed upon him, Adam formed a pretty fair notion of the degree of the young lady's gratitude. He found it interesting that although he had presented any number of costly geegaws to young females who had caught his fancy, not one of those barques of frailty had appeared as genuinely pleased with their diamonds or rubies as Miss Marianne McCord was with that creel of misbegotten felines.

Her eyes literally shone with pleasure. Watching her, Adam decided the half-mile walk across the back of their adjoining properties had been worth the effort.

Previously, he had thought his new neighbor no more than moderately pretty, but when she smiled at him, he was obliged to rethink that opinion. Her gray-green eyes sparkled like jewels, a complement to her complexion, which was a flawless peaches and cream, and her mouth, which was generous and full-lipped, was altogether kissable.

"Are they mine to keep?" she asked, forcing his thoughts from her tempting lips back to the cats. "Or shall I return them at some later date?"

"No, no. They are yours, Miss McCord. I cannot think that anyone at the Hall will mourn their loss."

"This is marvelous." Using her head to motion toward the kitchen door, she said, "Will you be so good as to bring the creel into the house for me?"

"Forgive me," Adam said, "I should have taken your packages."

"Never mind, I have them. Just get the creel."

Adam was hard pressed not to smile at this dust-covered nobody who thought nothing of issuing orders to one of the country's premier viscounts. Accustomed almost from the moment he gained his majority to being pursued and fawned upon by hopeful young ladies, he found it rather amusing that this one was more interested in a basket of cats than in gaining his attention.

"What of your horse?" he asked. "Should the . . . er, stubborn old nab girder be seen to?"

She gave him a telling look. "Sir, I wish you will forget you heard me utter that cant expression. As for the mare, it will do her no harm to wait for my return. You have my word upon it, never once did that bag of bones move fast enough to produce so much as a drop of sweat."

While Adam chuckled, the lady, who had obviously not meant to be entertaining, turned and walked rather purposefully toward the house, never doubting that he would follow. Adam was momentarily taken aback. He was no coxcomb, but neither was he given to false modesty. He knew that he was considered a matrimonial prize, and that any one of the young ladies in London would have considered herself in the running for his hand if he had laughed at something she had said.

Not so Miss Marianne McCord. Apparently, that damsel was unaware that she had scored a point with the most eligible bachelor in town. Unaware and—could it be?—uncaring. Retrieving the creel, Adam followed the lady into her house.

If the truth be known, he could not remember the last time he had been inside a kitchen, probably at some point in his boyhood, but as he entered the room and looked around, he knew for a fact he had never been in a dirtier kitchen than the one at Bibb Grange. What were the servants thinking of?

"Where is your housekeeper?" he asked, not bothering to hide his distaste at the state of the room.

"Gone," she replied. "Along with the cook and a male servant who tended the stable."

Avoiding his gaze, she set the packages on the wide deal table, removed the dark green spencer that was still covered with dust from her leap from the trap, then untied the strings of her small-poked straw bonnet. She placed the bonnet on a chair, then touched her hand to the hair that had escaped from the knot atop her head, trying in vain to make some order of a riot of loose curls.

Realizing the significance of what she had said about the servants, Adam asked rather abruptly, "Are you alone here? If you are, I warn you, it will not do. You cannot possibly remain here without—"

"Someone is coming this evening," she said, her voice noticeably cool. "A woman and her son."

As if to imply that the subject was closed, she took the creel from his hands, untied the rope, then lifted the lid. "Kittens! Oh, how adorable."

For his part, Adam saw nothing to admire in the thin, yellow-striped adult cat who lay curled in the bottom of the creel, her amber eyes trained on them suspiciously. As for the three kittens, he supposed they were taking enough, especially since none of the three resembled their parent. At the moment, they were asleep, lying atop one another, causing a blur of color that made it almost impossible to tell which tail belonged to which kitten.

One, a black with a white face and paws, bore a black marking above its tiny pink mouth—a marking that resembled a crooked mustache—while the second, the runt of the litter, was a mottled orange and black, the design resembling a tortoiseshell. The third, a solid gray with a fluffy coat, lifted its small head for a moment and peered at Adam, revealing rather pretty blue eyes.

"Will the mother let me pick them up?" Miss McCord asked.

Adam shrugged. "I know nothing of felines."

Moving slowly, Miss McCord reached over and ran one finger back and forth along the jawline of the adult cat, causing it to purr almost immediately. "Hello," she said as if speaking to a human. "I congratulate you upon your offspring, madam, for they are beautiful. May I touch them?"

The yellow cat, as if understanding the question, rose and stepped out of the creel onto the tabletop. After stretching her front legs and yawning wide enough to reveal a startling set of needle-sharp teeth, she jumped down to the floor and strolled toward the larder door, not bothering to look back.

Once the mother cat was out of the way, Miss McCord untangled one of the kittens—it turned out to be the one with the mustache—and placed it on her shoulder quite close to her neck. Uncaring that anyone was watching her, she nuzzled her cheek against the kitten's downy head, her eyes closed as if to heighten the sensation. "So soft," she murmured.

"I can believe it," Adam replied, his attention not on the kitten but on Marianne McCord's slender throat. Because she wore no fichu over the square neck of her dress, her throat and a goodly portion of her lovely bosom were exposed, prompting Adam to imagine how it would feel to rub his cheek against her soft, satiny skin.

She chose that moment to open her eyes, catching him looking at her, and for just a moment their gazes met and held. To Adam's surprise, she seemed unaware of the provocative picture she made and equally unaffected by his interest.

In this latter assumption, he was quite wrong, for when Marianne had looked up to discover the viscount watching her, she had experienced a decided flutter in her midsection. Unfortunately, his lordship's attention, though exciting, was also unsettling. Hoping to stamp out that fluttery sensation before it could take root and grow, Marianne reminded herself of the feeling she'd had when she first saw Lord Jenson at the Dog and Bear in Matlock the day before—a conviction that he was no gentleman.

From the moment he had looked at her, Marianne had known the man was dangerous. Those dark eyes saw too much, *knew* too much.

He was a man of the world. She did not need anyone to tell her that; she felt it instinctively. Just as she knew without question that he would be an expert in the ways of seduction. He was the sort of man her great-aunt had warned her about year after year—a man in possession of honeyed words and coaxing ways—and according to her great-aunt, Marianne was predisposed to be susceptible to just that sort of sweet-talker.

Not that Marianne believed her relative. If the truth be told, Marianne did not think she was any more susceptible than the next female. However, a woman with the least instinct for self-preservation would avoid a man like Viscount Jenson, avoid him at all costs. And she meant to do just that.

Resolving to be rid of the man as quickly as possible, she set the black-and-white kitten on the floor, then removed his two litter mates from the creel and set them on the floor as well. "Here you are, my lord," she said, holding the empty creel out to the viscount. "Thank you for the kittens."

"Actually," he said, ignoring the basket, "the kittens

were but an excuse. I came here for another reason entirely."

At his admission, that flutter returned to Marianne's midsection, accompanied by an odd mixture of excitement and apprehension. "Another reason?"

"Yes. To issue an apology."

She must have looked as confused as she felt, for he hurried to explain. "After the accident in the lane, which I realized later was not your fault, I called you an idiot. It was a thoughtless remark, Miss McCord, and I ask your pardon."

"Oh," she said, not certain if she was relieved or disappointed by his real reason for coming. "Think nothing of it, sir. Believe me, I have been called worse and lived to tell the tale."

"Have you now?" Lord Jenson's eyebrow rose in a teasing manner. "Like what?" he asked.

She shook her head. "Oh, no, my lord. I am not some green girl. I will not make you a gift of ready-made epithets with which to insult me. If at some time in the future you wish to rail at me, you will be obliged to find your own words."

"And what if I do not wish to rail at you?"

"Oh, you will, sir. Especially when you discover that I have already traded upon your name and rank."

It was his turn to look confused. "We met only a few hours ago. How, and where, could you possibly have traded upon our acquaintance?"

"In the village. One of the shopkeepers was less than amiable about filling my order, but when I mentioned your name, the fellow was all solicitude."

Her visitor was silent for a moment, then he said, "I hope you do not live to regret linking your name with mine."

"Why should I? Mentioning a member of the nobility is an *Open, Sesame* with tradesmen. I am wise to the ways of the world."

*"Au contraire,* madam. I am fast coming to the conclusion that you are like the little girl in the children's story—the girl in the red cape who went through the woods and met a wolf, then naively told him exactly where she was going and why."

After delivering that rather surprising observation, the viscount took the creel Marianne had offered him earlier and walked to the door. Just before he stepped outside, he turned back to look at her. "Miss McCord," he said, "I like you, and for that reason I shall extend to you a friendly warning."

"And what might that be?"

"You are a babe in the woods. You know it and I know it. Unfortunately, others are not so astute, and they are quick to judge. You are a woman alone, and association with me will not improve your reputation."

"You quite mistake the matter, sir. Alone I may be, but I will soon be six and twenty years old, and I am definitely not that naive girl in the red cape."

"Unfortunately," he said, "I *am* the big bad wolf. And you would do well not to forget it."


A full two hours later, when Hannah Scott arrived at Bibb Grange, Marianne was still musing over Lord Jenson's parting remark. Perhaps calling himself an animal of prey was a bit dramatic, but if the way he continued to occupy Marianne's thoughts was anything to go by, she might do well to remember his warning and keep her distance.

"Hello," someone called from just outside the open kitchen door. "Miss McCord? It's Hannah Scott."

Marianne had just poured herself a cup of tea, when she heard Hannah's voice. Making that tea had proven a difficult task. After several unsuccessful attempts to start a fire in the large stone fireplace, Marianne had finally succeeded in igniting the logs, and once the battered old copper kettle had come to the boil, she had added bohea and the steaming water to an ancient crockery pot, then set the pot aside to let the fragrant contents steep.

Upon hearing Hannah's greeting, Marianne delayed the first reviving sip of the mahogany-colored brew and hurried to the door, more pleased than she had thought possible to know she would not be spending a night alone at the grange.

"Come in," she said. "You are just in time for a cup of tea."

Hannah dropped a nervous curtsy, then stepped into the kitchen, her gaze taking in the room and her new employer, who sat at the table. Over her left arm Hannah Scott carried a large bundle tied up in a worn India shawl, and in her right hand she held the hand of a little boy whose bright red hair and blue eyes identified him as her son. She had said the boy was small for his age, and she was correct. Had Marianne not known his age to be twelve, she would have guessed him to be no more than ten years old.

His mother had been right, as well, about the lad being shy. From the moment he spied Marianne, the freckle-faced youngster gave his full attention to his rather scuffed footwear. He did not look up even when Hannah introduced him. "Make your bow to Miss

McCord," she said, and though the boy complied, he continued to regard his feet.

"Come," Marianne said to the mother, indicating a chair on the other side of the freshly scrubbed table.

Though Hannah took the chair, the tight lacing of her fingers gave evidence of her apparent discomfort at being in her new employer's presence.

"May I pour you a cup of bohea?"

"No, thank you, miss. Georgie and me had a bite before we left the cottage."

"Georgie," Marianne said, "you may come sit with your mother and me, or you may take her bundle into the room just to the right off the corridor." When the boy picked up the bundle, Marianne warned him to open the door carefully. "You will find a basket at the foot of the bed. I set it in your mother's room while I had the kitchen door open, for I did not want the occupants of the basket to wander outside."

His curiosity finally overcoming his shyness, the boy looked up, a question in his eyes, but his mother told him to do as he was bid.

"You may come back here whenever you wish," Marianne said. As soon as he was out of sight, she whispered to his mother, "I hope he likes kittens."

At the question, Hannah relaxed her death grip on her fingers. "He does, miss. And anything else on four legs. He's a pure fool about animals. Got a real way with them has my Georgie."

"I am delighted to hear it, for I cannot help but think highly of people who are kind to God's lesser creatures."

Hannah smiled and appeared to relax at last. "Georgie'll be a real help in the stable one day. I grant he's a mite small right now to take care of a spirited horse, but if you're willing to give him a try, I believe he can tend that old mare that pulled the trap."

"But what of his schooling? I understood there was a school in the village."

"There was used to be, miss. But not no more. I went there myself for two years, but when my mam died giving birth to Willem, I had to stay home to look after Papa and the bairn. While I was at the school, though, I learned to read and write a little, and do sums, so I've taught Georgie as much as I know."

During Marianne's first look at the village, she had realized the mill and the houses had seen better days, but she was genuinely disappointed to hear that the school had been closed. "What happened? About the school, I mean. Do you know?"

"All I know, miss, is what we were told. 'Course, things started going down in the mill and the village soon after the old viscount died and his son inherited. Repairs weren't made to cottages, and those that were seen to were only half done. Even so, the school was kept open until six years ago."

"What happened six years ago?"

"That was when the old viscount's grandson inherited."

For some reason, at the mention of the newest viscount, Marianne felt her face grow warm. He might be the big bad wolf he had said he was, but Marianne disliked thinking the same Lord Jenson who had brought her the kittens had ordered the school closed. "Are you certain the viscount wished this done?"

"Bob Quimby, him as is the mill superintendent, said it was the new owner's wishes. According to Quimby, he was just following orders when he let the teachers go. 'Course, we've only his word for that."

From the way Hannah spoke, Marianne gained the impression that her new housekeeper did not trust the superintendent. "Do you think he was lying?"

"I can't say for sure, miss, but I wouldn't put anything past Bob Quimby if there was tuppence in it for him." She shuddered, and though she tried to hide the fact, Marianne noticed.

"You do not like this Quimby fellow, do you?"

"I don't, and that's a fact."

"May I ask why?"

Hannah hesitated only a moment. "His wife died last spring, and the diggers had only just finished shoveling the earth over her casket, when Quimby started coming around the cottage, making up to me and bringing me little gifts and such. As if I'd have anything to do with the likes of him." Her lip curled in distaste. "At least Georgie's papa was a gentleman, and not some lout with dirt under his fingernails."

*At least?*

Marianne was not surprised to hear that the boy's father was a gentleman, for so-called gentlemen left their by-blows all over the countryside, but that slip of the tongue—that *at least*—explained more than Hannah Scott might wish to tell. Keeping her suspicions regarding Georgie's conception to herself, Marianne asked what happened with Quimby.

"I refused his gifts and his invitations to walk out with him. Of course, I tried to be polite about my refusal, seeing as how my papa and my brother both work in the mill. But I might as well have saved my breath, for Quimby wouldn't take no for an answer."

She glanced toward the corridor where her son had gone, then lowered her voice. "One night Quimby came by the cottage while Papa and Willem were visiting a sick neighbor. When he found out the menfolk were gone and that we were alone, he started pawing me and trying to coax me out to the barn. I told him to leave me be and to go home, but he didn't do either. Finally, I was obliged to box his ears."

She paused for a moment. "Bob Quimby b'aint one as takes rebuff kindly. It's his two boys as are bullying my Georgie, and I'm certain their papa put them up to it." Hannah's blue eyes flashed with anger. "He looks down his nose at my son, like it was Georgie committed the sin instead of me."

As memories flooded back to Marianne, memories of others who looked down their noses, she was obliged to swallow to release the tightness that gripped her throat. "People can be cruel," she said. "And the way I see it, there is no greater sin than being cruel to a child."

Nothing more was said on the subject of Bob Quimby, for Georgie returned at that moment. His arms were filled with kittens, and the mesmerized mother cat followed close behind him much as the rats of Hamlin must have followed the Pied Piper. A shy smile lit the boy's freckled face. "They like me," he said. Then, rather softly, "Can I have one, Mama?"

Hannah looked from her son to Marianne, a question in her eyes.

"Perhaps," Marianne said in reply to the woman's unspoken question, "you should look around the grange before you decide whether or not you truly wish to be in my employ. A lot of work needs to be done around here."

"A bit of dirt don't frighten me, miss. If you'll have us, we'd like to stay."

Marianne breathed a sigh of relief. "In that case,

Georgie, you had better start thinking of suitable names, for once the mother cat weans them, all three kittens are yours."

# Four

Marianne did not see the viscount again for more than a week. As a matter of fact, she and Hannah worked practically nonstop, scrubbing the house from kitchen to attic, airing the bedding from the six bedrooms, and searching through years' worth of stored linens and mismatched tableware. Often they paused only long enough to eat whatever was easiest to prepare. The entire cleaning frenzy was a labor of love, however, for both women worked to make the grange their home.

At last, when every room was clean and each worn item either set aside to be mended or discarded, they brought down from the attic a few pieces of furniture dating from the past century. Among the pieces that had been stacked like so much trash was a beautiful old Queen Anne writing desk fashioned of walnut. Some foreign object had become wedged in the single drawer, which refused to open; nevertheless, the simple design of the desk and the matching splat-back chair appealed to Marianne. Once the items were cleaned and waxed, she moved them into the master bedchamber.

That chamber had undergone a drastic change, beginning with the removal of a leather barbering chair and continuing with the weeding-out of several heavy, serviceable tables that had been deemed suitable for a sick-room. After Marianne had taken down the ornate wine-velvet window and bed hangings and let in the light, the chamber and adjoining dressing room were revealed as a very handsome apartment.

Marianne's favorite place, however, was the blue-and-white parlor just off the vestibule. The room contained a large fireplace with a frieze of roses above the carved oak mantelpiece and a charming inglenook with blue-and-white chintz upholstery on the two benches. To the right stood a glass-fronted vitrine, and beside the vitrine was a tilt-top rosewood worktable. Marianne sat at the worktable, going over her finances, when Hannah tapped at the door.

"Come in," she said, looking up from the small ledger she had purchased to help her keep a record of her expenditures. Mrs. Fannon's warning had proven true, for during the rain of the previous day the roof had, indeed, leaked in several places. As for the four double chimneys in the house, there was not one that did not belch smoke back into the rooms. Regrettably, the fireplace in the master bedchamber smoked so badly, it had discolored a rather charming family portrait that hung over the mantelpiece.

At some date in the near future, when Marianne had taken care of all the other needed repairs, she hoped to find someone who could clean and restore the painting, which was sixty to seventy years old. Unless she missed her guess, the little boy in short coats, who posed with twin girls of about six or seven years and a pretty woman dressed in panniers and an elaborate powdered wig, was Mr. Theodore Bibb. Treating the painting with respect was one way Marianne could thank the old gentleman for bequeathing Bibb Grange to her mother.

"If my figures are correct," Marianne began the moment Hannah entered the room, "I have enough money left to see to the patching of the roof. As for the chimneys, they will have to wait until next quarter day." She lifted her hand to reveal crossed fingers. "Let us pray for a late autumn."

"That was what I came in to talk to you about, miss. Praying."

Marianne must have looked as confused as she felt, for Hannah said, "You may not have realized it, us being so busy and all this past week, but it's the Sabbath. Again. We missed service last week, but unless I'm abed with some ailment, I always attend. Me and Georgie both."

She colored slightly and looked down at her feet, reminding Marianne of the shy Georgie. "I don't know if the Lord still believes in me, miss, but I believe in Him."

"Of course you do."

Marianne was no expert on religious matters, but she had been given firm principles as a child. Thankfully, almost ten years of her great-aunt's sanctimonious zeal had not been enough to shake her confidence in the Heavenly Father's unconditional love.

"Old Mr. Bibb had a pew," Hannah said, "though he didn't use it much those last two years. Still, it's there, and if you've a mind to go to services, Georgie and me will wait while you get dressed."

By the time Hannah had finished her offer, even her ears were red with embarrassment. "Begging your pardon, miss, if I've given offense."

"From the moment you walked into this house, Hannah Scott, you've given me nothing but good advice. Now advise me again. What shall I wear? I'll need something subdued enough not to scandalize the pious yet bright enough to let those who would snub me know that I will not be intimidated."

Hannah nodded her approval. "That's what I thought, miss, so I took the liberty of pressing your jonquil frock. With the bronze-color pelisse and the matching tussore silk bonnet, you should do nicely."

The bronze pelisse and bonnet were Marianne's best, and though perhaps not up to London's exacting measure of style, they should be deemed fashionable enough by the standards of the villagers. One quick glance in the looking glass was enough to convince Marianne that finery was just the thing to give her courage for her second trip to Chelmford. Once she had fastened the gold chain around her neck and tucked the filigree fob inside the collar of the jonquil frock, she hurried down the stairs, out the kitchen door, and to the stable. To her surprise, she found Georgie standing proudly beside the mare he had harnessed to the trap.

"Why, Georgie. Did you see to Bess all by yourself?"

Like his mother, the boy blushed all over, but at least he had grown accustomed enough to Marianne to mumble an affirmative reply. "She's a good girl, is Bess."

Though that assessment was debateable, Marianne chose not to argue the point; instead, she merely climbed aboard the trap and lifted the ribbons. Hannah and her son took their places in the other half of the divided seat, and soon the three of them were on their way to the village.

Marianne had told Hannah about her encounter with the viscount, when his horse had jumped over the trap, so when Bess plodded past the spot where it had occurred, Marianne pointed to the place his lordship had landed in the dusty lane. "It was just there," she said.

"Actually," countered a deep voice she was coming to recognize, "I believe it was a bit farther to the right."

"Lord Jenson!" Marianne turned to find him on the other side of the low stone wall, astride a rather nondescript chestnut. "I did not see you, sir."

"Again? Tell me, madam, are you in need of spectacles?"

"First you must tell me, sir, if your purpose in waiting there—in ambush, as it were—was to see if you could successfully jump over the trap this time."

Hannah gasped, but his lordship chuckled. "On this poor excuse for a horse? Not likely, Miss McCord. I fear this fellow is destined to join the ranks of that high-stepper you drive."

"High-stepper? If you refer to Bess, perhaps it is you, sir, who wants spectacles."

Lord Jenson vouchsafed no reply, for the maligned mare had continued her slow pace, leaving him with no recourse but to tip his hat and bid them good day.

"Shall we see you at the service?" Marianne called over her shoulder.

"No," he replied, raising his voice to be heard. "If I should walk into a church, the very foundations would tremble and the roof would probably collapse. Better for all concerned if I stay away, for I am definitely on the devil's list."

Though Marianne smiled, she did not look back, and soon she become lost in thought, mulling over the brief meeting with Lord Jenson. Several minutes passed before she was roused from her reverie, and only then did she notice that Hannah sat very straight, her attention focused on her folded hands. "Hannah? Is something amiss?"

At first Marianne thought her new employee meant

not to reply. After several moments, however, she said, "It's about the gentleman."

"The gentleman? Do you refer to the viscount? What about him?"

She hesitated again. "Never mind, miss. I should not have spoken."

"Of course you should have, and I wish you will continue."

As though choosing her words carefully, she said, "If you'll forgive me for saying so, miss, it b'aint wise to be bantering with the likes of such a man."

Marianne had enjoyed the banter with Lord Jenson, but at Hannah's warning, some of her enjoyment faded. On the defensive, she said, "The viscount is my neighbor. I could hardly ignore him."

"No need to ignore him, but a simple nod would have sufficed."

After spending time with each other on two previous occasions, she and Adam Jenson were well past the simple nodding stage. Unfortunately, Marianne could not expect Hannah to appreciate how quickly and naturally all formality had ceased between them.

"Anything more, miss, and he's like to get ideas."

"What sort of ideas?"

Hannah looked meaningfully toward her son, as if to remind Marianne that the lad was listening to their every word. "You know the kind of ideas gentlemen get when they see a pretty female. And he said himself that he's on the devil's list."

"You cannot have believed him. Why, the comment was made in jest."

Still uncharacteristically stiff, Hannah said, "All I know, miss, is there's truth in drink and there's truth in jest. Besides, rumor has it that where the ladies are concerned, his lordship's a bit of a devil himself."

Marianne did not dignify that particular rumor with a reply, and the remainder of the trip was completed in strained silence. It was one thing for Lord Jenson to call himself names, but it annoyed Marianne no end to hear someone else speak ill of him. It should not have, of course, for though she had found herself imagining his handsome face, and especially those dark, teasing eyes on more than one occasion this past week, in truth he was practically a stranger to her. And yet, he had been kind, and she tried never to judge people by the standards set by others.

For some reason, Hannah had obviously taken the viscount in dislike, and Marianne, unable to discern why, was relieved when they finally reached the stone bridge that crossed the mill pond. They said no more as they passed the mill and Wethington's shop, then continued along the high street to the church.

Though Marianne had been dreading the solitary walk down the aisle to Theodore Bibb's private pew, knowing full well that every eye would be on her, she soon discovered that taking her place in the enclosure just to the right of the pulpit was easy. What had been difficult was enduring the strained silence that had prevailed between her and Hannah during the remainder of the drive through the village.

Once they entered the handsome limestone church with its polished oak wainscoting and its tracery windows, Hannah and Georgie joined Willem and Mr. Scott at the back of the sanctuary, leaving Marianne to walk alone to the Bibb private pew. Though the sides of the enclosure were high enough to offer her a degree of privacy when she was seated, each time the congregation stood to sing a hymn, Marianne was in full view, and she felt the stares of the parishioners behind her.

She had not expected to be greeted with open arms, but neither had she anticipated the frigid reception she received from the villagers as they filed out of the church following the service. No one was openly rude, but each time Marianne made eye contact with someone, they looked away quickly, making a show of gathering a forgotten prayer book or hurrying a dawdling child. It was that display of coolness that prompted Marianne to smile favorably upon a plump though fashionably dressed gentleman who approached her once she was outside the sanctuary.

Knowing that Hannah and Georgie paid a visit to Mrs. Scott's grave each Sunday, Marianne found a spot to wait for them—a spot somewhat apart from the parishioners who congregated near a pair of hawthorn bushes whose thick, green-leafed branches had been allowed to grow to perhaps twenty feet. She was trying not to eavesdrop on friendly exchanges between neighbors, when the gentleman spoke her name.

"Miss McCord?"

His greeting surprised her into turning toward him, a smile on her face. "Yes?"

"Good day," he said, doffing the tan curly-brimmed beaver that complemented his snug-fitting ocher coat and saffron-colored inexpressibles. "May I beg a moment of your time?"

The man was short, no more than an inch or two taller than Marianne, and his sandy-brown hair was combed into a Brutus that did not suit his fleshy face. In his mid-thirties, he might once have been handsome, but now his mouth bore a rather petulant expression and his gray eyes looked about him with a certain disdain for all he saw.

Under ordinary circumstances, had a man approached her without a proper introduction, Marianne would have given him the snub he deserved. But not today. Today she felt rather alone, standing there amid her unfriendly new neighbors, so she returned the gentleman's smile and allowed him to introduce himself.

"I am Titus Brougham," he said. "Titus *Bibb* Brougham."

Though surprised to hear the name, Marianne offered him her hand, then waited while he bowed over it. "Are you related to Mr. Theodore Bibb, sir, the former owner of Bibb Grange?"

"I have that honor, ma'am. He was the younger brother of my mother and her twin sister."

"Then you . . . you are his nephew?"

"That honor, also, is mine."

A nephew! Marianne could not think what to say, and as she stood there, staring into Mr. Brougham's smiling face, she felt the warmth of embarrassment steel up her neck, knowing that she—and not some relative—had inherited Bibb Grange. From the moment she had received the letter informing her that she was the new owner of the property, she had assumed that Mr. Theodore Bibb had gone to his heavenly reward leaving no living relatives. Otherwise, why would he bequeath his property to a stranger rather than to someone of his own blood?

Of course, Marianne could think of no reasonable explanation for his leaving the grange to her mother in the first place. The bequest was something of a mystery, for as far as Marianne could determine, Daisy McCord had no connection whatever to Theodore Bibb, nor had she ever had an occasion to meet the gentleman. Now, here was a relative—a *male* relative—of the previous owner's, and Marianne felt more confused than ever.

"Were you acquainted with Mr. Bibb?" she asked, hoping the family were not on good terms.

"Oh, yes," Mr. Brougham replied, effectively shattering that possible explanation. "I escorted my mother to Chelmford a number of years ago. We remained at the grange with my uncle for the better part of a fortnight."

"Then you and he got along?"

"I was only just down from university, but if memory serves, ours was a pleasant enough visit. I remember my uncle as a rather reclusive old fellow but likable for all that."

The mystery grew. If family animosity did not account for the fact that the property did not pass to Mr. Brougham, then what possible reason could the gentleman's uncle have had for naming Daisy McCord his beneficiary?

Swallowing with difficulty, Marianne asked the question that was gnawing at her, making her knees tremble. "Sir," she said, "you will forgive me if I appear too inquisitive, but have you, perchance, come to Chelmford to contest your uncle's will?"

"Contest the will?" Mr. Brougham waved a negligent hand. "Not at all, dear lady. Why, the notion never entered my mind. 'Tis a small property, after all, and hardly worth my notice."

Marianne let go the breath she had not realized she held. A small property it might be, but the grange meant the world to her. She loved it. Even stronger than her love for the place, however, was her fear for her future. Without the grange and the two hundred pounds per annum that came with it, where would she go? How would she support herself?"

"I am come to Derbyshire," Mr. Brougham continued, a practiced smile appearing upon his face, "on an entirely different matter. Before I left town, my uncle's man of business, Mr. Penell, informed me that you had written him of your plans to take up residence at the grange right away, so while I was in the neighborhood— I am staying at the Swan, by the way—I thought merely to avail myself of the opportunity to make your acquaintance."

"How . . . how kind of you, sir."

They spoke for several minutes, with the gentleman sharing with her two or three of his memories of his previous stay at the grange, but as soon as Marianne could excuse herself without giving offense, she told him that she needed to find her housekeeper. Somehow, Mr. Brougham's reminiscences had a rehearsed sound to them, and Marianne had begun to feel uneasy in his company.

After a polite curtsy, she said, "Happy to have met you, sir. I hope your present stay in Derbyshire is enjoyable."

"Actually," he said, stopping her retreat with a word she suspected meant the speaker was about to recant his previous statement, "I mean to be in the vicinity for at least another week. Perhaps we shall meet again, Miss McCord."

Without committing herself, she said, "Good day, sir."

Apparently taking his second dismissal in good part, he smiled again and tipped his hat politely. "Good day, ma'am."

For some reason, Marianne felt a quite illogical desire to lift her skirts and run from Titus Brougham's presence. He had said everything that was proper, and she could find no fault in his manner, and yet, there was something about him she could not like. Perhaps it was that practiced smile—a smile that did not quite reach his eyes. More logically, it was the threat he represented to her future, never mind his assurances to the contrary.

Though she did not obey the impulse to run, Marianne allowed herself to walk with slightly quickened steps toward the churchyard where Hannah's mother lay buried. Upon spying Hannah and Georgie, their flame-haired heads bowed in prayer, Marianne paused near a tallish headstone adorned with a pair of angels. After stepping around the headstone so that she was out of sight of Mr. Brougham, she peered over the angels' wings to see if he was still there, watching her.

He was there, but he was in conversation with a blond young lady whose greater height required the gentleman to look up. Relieved that he appeared to have lost all interest in her, Marianne exhaled rather loudly.

"What's amiss?" Hannah asked.

The woman's unexpected nearness caused Marianne to turn rather more quickly than she had meant, and she was obliged to grab hold of one of the angels to keep from falling. "Oh, Hannah! You startled me."

"Your pardon, I'm sure, miss, but you looked for all the world like you were hiding. I thought maybe someone had said summit to you."

"Nothing to signify. I was just looking at that man over there with the tall blond lady. The one—" When she turned to point out Mr. Brougham to Hannah, he was no longer there. The young lady was alone.

"Miss Havor, do you mean, miss?"

With the man no longer in sight, Marianne felt a bit foolish for having acted like the veriest ninnyhammer, so she bid Hannah forget the matter entirely. "If you are ready, I should like to go home."

*Home. What a wonderful word.*

Marianne may have been in residence at the grange for only ten days, but it was her home now, and if Mr. Titus Brougham thought to try to take it from her, he would find he had a battle on his hands. Of course, he had said he had come to Derbyshire for another purpose, but somehow Marianne did not believe him. Never mind his fashionable clothes and his polite manners, she did not trust him. Not for a minute. Unless she missed her guess, he was the type of man who took what he wanted and cared little who got hurt as a result.

"There's Georgie with the trap," Hannah said. "Let's go home."

Later that afternoon, Marianne still had not rid herself of her concern that Titus Brougham might attempt to disrupt her newfound happiness. Hoping that fresh air would clear her head, she decided to have a look at the grounds beyond the weed-choked kitchen garden and the stables. During the past week and a half, she had been too busy with the house to give much thought to the estate, but now she wanted to see a bit of what had been left to her by Mr. Theodore Bibb.

After donning a pair of walking boots and throwing an old paisley shawl over an equally old blue sprigged muslin, Marianne went belowstairs, her object to tell Hannah that she would be gone from home for a while. When she passed through the kitchen, she found her new housekeeper sitting beside the fireplace, a large, worn Bible open across her lap. She waited until Hannah came to a stopping place and rested her finger along one of scrolled pages. "Yes, miss?"

"I am going for a walk, but I shall return within the hour."

"Very well, miss. If you see ought of Georgie, please tell him to come home. He knows he's to stay close by on the Sabbath."

Marianne agreed to deliver the message, then she stepped outside and walked rather briskly toward the wood beyond the stables. A footpath worn by who-knew-how-many feet led her up a slight incline into the wood, which was thick with tall beech trees—trees that reached to the sky like cathedral columns. Because of the dense shade beneath those beeches, little vegetation grew on the earth's floor save dark green moss and a few wood anemones that peeped their purple-blue heads up where stray shafts of sun dared to dapple the springy ground.

All about her was peace and beauty, and they filled Marianne's heart and calmed her soul.

To her right, a pair of bushy-tailed red squirrels chased each other up one tree and down another, their agitated chirps and whistles sounding loud in the hushed wood. While to her left, a yellow-throated nuthatch took flight, its blue wings soon taking it above the treetops and out of sight.

Marianne had traversed no more than half a mile, lost in the beauty of the wood, when she was brought up short by the sound of voices. Though surprised, she was not frightened, for she recognized both speakers immediately. The child's high-pitched voice belonged to Georgie Scott, while the smooth, mellow baritone belonged to their neighbor, Lord Jenson.

"He needs help," Georgie said. "What do you think I should do, sir?"

Keeping her steps soft, Marianne approached a dwarfed service tree not far from the two speakers, where she could remain out of sight yet peep around the bole of the tree to assure herself that all was well. She felt a certain responsibility for Georgie, but she did not wish him to feel he could not wander freely about the property.

When she saw the boy, his hands were cupped close together, as if he held something small in them. He was looking up in a worshipful manner at the tall gentleman who stood not two feet away, his attention on whatever the boy held in his hands. "Shall I climb the tree, my lord, and put the little bird back in the nest? I'm not afraid to climb, really I'm not."

Marianne gasped, for the bird's nest, which was visible, was perched on a limb perhaps thirty feet off the ground. Aware that a fall from that height might prove fatal, she was trying to think how to stop Georgie from committing such a foolish act, hopefully without hurting the shy child's feelings, when Lord Jenson spoke quietly.

"Yours is a brave offer, lad, but I do not think a climb is called for. Actually, it might be wisest if you set the fledgling there at the base of the tree, where his mother can see him. I assure you, she will hear his call and come looking for him."

When Georgie hesitated, the viscount gave the boy's thin shoulder a reassuring squeeze. "It is usually best, lad, if humans do not interfere with the creatures of the forest. Though we mean well, invariably we do the wrong thing."

While Marianne listened to Adam Jenson's advice and watched him put his hand on Georgie's shoulder, the gesture surprisingly fatherly, she had the oddest sensation, almost as if she could feel a masculine hand on *her* shoulder. Foolish, of course, for she had no idea what it was like to have a father, or how it felt to have a male's guiding touch. She never had, and she never would.

Marianne swallowed an obstruction in her throat—an obstruction whose cause she did not wish to consider—then she watched Georgie do as the viscount had suggested. The lad placed the tiny bird at the base of the tree, and while the two males gave their attention to the wild creature, Marianne stepped from behind her hiding place.

Dispensing with a greeting, she said, "Ah, Georgie. Here you are."

Man and boy turned as one, both surprised to see her.

"Were you looking for me, miss?"

"Yes. I have a message from your mother."

The boy's face turned a deep red, and he stole a glance at the tall gentleman beside him. When he spoke, his boyish voice betrayed his typically male embarrassment at having been summoned by his mother. "She wants me home for Sabbath reading."

"And not a minute too soon," the viscount said, giving the boy a wink. "Who knows what mischief we might have gotten up to if you had lingered another hour."

Being a shy boy, Georgie was not given to exuberant expression, so his smile was that much sweeter for its rarity. "Thank you, sir," he said, "for the help with the bird."

"My pleasure, lad."

Georgie raised his hand in salute, then turned and

retraced his steps, his destination the footpath that led to the grange. The moment he was out of hearing, Marianne added her thanks to his. "You were very good, my lord, to keep Georgie from doing something dangerous, while allowing him to maintain his pride."

When the viscount made as if to deny having done anything, Marianne would not let him finish. "Georgie is small for his age, and he is being hounded by a pair of village bullies. I feared he might try to climb the tree in hopes of proving his mettle. Thankfully, you handled the situation with real diplomacy."

"Believe it or not, Miss McCord, I was a child once myself, with a child's vulnerability."

Unable to picture the tall, muscular man before her as anything but assured and in control, she said, "You were a *child*? Forgive me, sir, but are not wolf offspring called pups?"

Though he did not smile, his eyes betrayed his amusement. "So, you remembered my warning."

"How could I not, my lord? It is not every day a gentleman tells me he is a man-eating beast."

"Not *man*-eating," he said.

As he spoke, he looked her over from her head to her boots, in a lazy manner that sent ripples of sensation to every spot his gaze had touched. "Your woman's intuition must tell you that these lips prefer flesh that is soft and satiny."

Marianne had no great faith in intuition, especially not when she was finding it so difficult to draw an even breath. Furthermore, something was causing the pulse in her neck to beat wildly. She suspected the culprit was the viscount's softly spoken words, for they contained a husky quality that intensified the image already in her mind of his lips touching *her* skin.

*Heaven help me! Great-aunt Gertrude was correct. I am susceptible to men with honeyed words and coaxing ways.*

Not wanting Lord Jenson to see the effect he had upon her, Marianne turned away, pretending to look at the small bird Georgie had set at the base of the tree. "Will the mother return, do you think?"

"I suspect she is watching even now, waiting for us to move away so she might come to her chick."

The words said, he touched Marianne's elbow and led her some distance away, stopping only when they came upon a coppiced tree. After suggesting that she take advantage of the forest "stool," he surprised her by placing his hands on either side of her waist and lifting her so she could sit upon what remained of the tree.

Once she was settled, he asked her why she was so far from the grange, with no one to protect her from chance-met predators. "Of course, I am always pleased to see a friendly face, but at the moment, the lady behind that face appears a bit distracted."

Marianne *was* distracted; she had been for the past half hour. Beginning with the unexpected sight of the viscount's gentle handling of Georgie and ending with the way her heart had skipped a beat when Adam Jenson lifted her onto the coppiced tree, as if she weighed no more than a kitten. Most of all, though, she was distracted by her growing fear that she was proving vulnerable to the viscount's charms.

Unwilling to give voice to those disturbing thoughts, she chose to answer his first question. "I am in the wood, my lord, because I needed a long walk. I had hoped the fresh air might help me think through something that happened at church."

The viscount feigned shock. "Never tell me the

church roof collapsed after all, even though I stayed away."

"In a manner of speaking, it did fall. For me, at least."

At her words, all teasing vanished from the viscount's expression, and he looked at Marianne as if waiting for her to continue. Hoping he might be able to tell her something of Theodore Bibb's nephew, she said, "Are you acquainted with a man named Titus Brougham?"

"Brougham? I know *of* him. He and I do not travel in the same circles, but occasionally our paths cross when we are in London. Mostly, we meet at the gaming tables. Why do you ask?"

"I met him today after the service. He introduced himself to me."

" 'Tis the kind of thing he *would* do. Poor *ton,* of course, to foist himself upon a lady without a proper introduction, but I cannot see anything so earth-shattering about being obliged to exchange civilities with the fellow in full view of the congregation."

"Except that he introduced himself as the nephew of the previous owner of Bibb Grange, and until that moment, I had not known that Theodore Bibb had any relatives."

"And now?"

Marianne hesitated a moment, feeling a bit foolish giving voice to her fears. "And now I wonder why Mr. Titus Brougham chose this time to come to Chelmford. I cannot help but think he may wish to contest the will. Of course, he denied any such plan, but I did not believe him."

To her relief, the viscount did not make light of her suspicions, but said only, "I had not thought the grange large enough to interest a man of Brougham's apparently expensive taste. Is it such a desirable estate?"

"It is to me! Aside from providing me with a home of my own, there is a legacy in the amount of two hundred pounds per annum."

With no wish to insult the lady, who obviously considered two hundred pounds a princely sum, Adam Jenson refrained from informing her that he had been known to spend that amount on a single pair of well-made top boots. Furthermore, he was willing to wager that Titus Brougham did the same.

Though Adam had no fondness for Brougham and men of his ilk—men who moved in less elevated circles of society and who lived pretty much by their wits—he acquitted the fellow of coveting an insignificant estate and what amounted to pocket change.

Striving to be tactful, he said, "I know that Brougham is given to deep play at the gaming tables, but if he is under the hatches, I cannot think an estate the size of Bibb Grange would satisfy even a portion of his debt. For such a man, his best hope of coming about is to marry an heiress. One," Adam added, "with at least ten or fifteen thousand."

Marianne remained silent for a time, as if considering his words, then shook her head. "What you say sounds reasonable enough, my lord, and yet, something tells me I should be wary of Mr. Titus Brougham. You may choose to think me naive, but something—perhaps it is an instinct for survival—warns me that this man could bring my new life crashing down about my ears."

A slight trembling of her pretty mouth told Adam that Miss Marianne McCord was not overstating her concerns. In an effort to convince her that all might not be lost if the will were contested, he said, "Is your situ-

ation truly so grievous? If you should lose the grange,
surely you could return to the great-aunt you mentioned
when first we met."

To Adam's surprise, the lady's gray-green eyes flashed
with angry resolve. "That bridge has been burned, my
lord. And even if it had not, I would not cross it again."

"I see." He did not see, of course, but he understood
enough of families to know that some relationships were
intolerable. "Is she your only relative? Have you no
other to whom you might turn?"

At his question, Miss McCord donned a sort of protective mask—a remote look that dared anyone to probe
further into her private life—and though Adam could
not understand why it should be so, he knew he had
stumbled upon a sensitive issue. "Forgive me," he said,
"if my questions are officious."

"I have a grandfather," she said, her voice sounding
dispassionate, as though she spoke of someone other
than herself.

"A *grandfather!*" Adam could not stop the inflection
in his voice, for he found it difficult to believe that any
man would allow his granddaughter to fend for herself.

"Yes," she replied in that same almost-disinterested
voice. "My grandfather's name is Sir Hyram McCord."

"*General* Sir Hyram McCord?"

She nodded.

In an attempt to hide his surprise at the information
that her grandfather was none other than the hero of
Montreal, in the war with the colonists, Adam said, "I
am acquainted with Sir Hyram. Only slightly, of course,
for he was my father's contemporary. Still, I have been
in company with him more than once, and in that time
he never mentioned having a son."

If possible, that protective mask the lady had donned

appeared even more impenetrable. "He does not, my lord."

"But you just said that your grandfather—"

"McCord is my mother's name."

As if daring him to snub her, she said, "I am someone's *natural* daughter."

# Five

"They eloped," she said, concluding the brief story of the seventeen-year-old Daisy McCord's romance with the twenty-year-old Lieutenant Marcus Wilson.

"Because of their ages, my grandfather was able to have the marriage set aside, and within days he saw to it that the lieutenant was sent to Barbados. My mother was heartbroken, for the young couple was very much in love."

She paused, and when she spoke again, her voice was hushed, as if relating the next part of the story were difficult. "It was only later that Daisy discovered she was with child."

Adam could only guess how much the telling of this story cost his neighbor, and though he did not wish to add to her embarrassment, he spoke before he thought. "Could the lieutenant not have been brought home and a second wedding ceremony arranged? Under those circumstances, surely it served no purpose to keep them apart, regardless of their youth."

She gave him a look that said he was being obtuse. "It served the general's purpose, my lord, for he had already chosen a wealthy nabob for his daughter to marry."

"But if she was with child—"

"A mere inconvenience. My grandfather's plan was to send my mother away privately for her confinement. After the delivery, she was supposed to give her baby to a couple the general had paid, then she was to return home and accept the nabob's marriage proposal. Needless to say, she refused to give me away."

"She was very brave, a girl of seventeen."

"Very. Unfortunately, the general does not admire bravery in females. In fact, he despises opposition of any kind. As you can imagine, when my mother refused to do as he commanded, he washed his hands of her."

"But what of you? What of his grandchild?"

Though she shrugged as if the matter were of no importance, Adam was not deceived; the slight trembling of her lower lip gave the lie to her pretended indifference.

"As far as the general is concerned, I do not exist."

She paused once again, this time to take a deep breath, as though the remainder of the story were more difficult to tell than the first. "After my mother's death, I wrote the general a letter advising him of the passing of his only child. I received no reply to my missive."

"No reply! Nothing at all?"

"At least nothing in writing. A week later, the general's man of business came and took me to Wales."

"To your great-aunt."

"Yes, to the general's sister, Gertrude Posner. But before you pin a medal on my only other living relative, allow me to inform you that she received money each month—how much I do not know—for taking me into her home. The general's only stipulation to her, that I was never to contact him again."

Adam could find nothing to say that did not involve words unfit for a lady's ears, so he asked her if her

mother had ever heard from the lieutenant after he was
sent to Barbados. "Did she never inform him, or his
family, of your existence?"

"If he had any family, my mother knew nothing of
them. As for Lieutenant Marcus Wilson, he succumbed
to a fever during his first year in the tropics. The general sent my mother only one letter after she refused to
give me up, and that was to apprise her of my father's
death."

Often during her story, Miss McCord had reached up
and touched some sort of little gold trinket at her neck,
as if drawing strength from the contact. She touched it
once again, and when she spoke, her voice was suspiciously husky. "My mother never got over the heartache
of knowing that the only man she had ever loved was
lost to her forever."

Adam had never allowed himself to become involved
in other people's problems, but it infuriated him that a
self-centered old man would ruin his daughter's happiness and brand his grandchild with the stigma of illegitimacy. Soon, Adam's anger gave way to an
unlooked-for wish to fold Marianne McCord in his arms
and tell her that all would be well . . . that he would
see to it that all was well.

Naturally, he did nothing of the kind.

There were only two ways a single man could take
care of a female. He might marry her, a solution that
did not appeal at all to a confirmed bachelor, or he
might take her for his mistress. For Adam Jenson, the
latter was a far more palatable alternative.

Actually, when he thought about it, the idea was not
half bad. He *liked* Marianne McCord, and that was more
than he could say for the majority of the people of his
acquaintance.

Of course, she was no match for the sort of stunning female he was accustomed to taking under his protection, but she was a pretty creature, with that thick brown hair and those saucy gray-green eyes. As for her figure, though she made no effort to show it to advantage, she had curves enough to appeal to any man, even one as jaded as Adam Jenson.

Allowing his thoughts free rein, Adam imagined her lying upon silk sheets, her hair loose about her shoulders and her tantalizing body covered only by a thin, lace-edged night rail. She would be waiting for him, a smile upon her lips, and her soft, satiny arms beckoning him to come to her . . . to take her in his arms and cover her mouth with his . . . to introduce her to the mysteries of—

"Lord Jenson!" she said, putting an end to an unexpectedly delightful fantasy and bringing his thoughts back to her present problem. "You seemed a million miles away. What on earth were you thinking?"

Looking into that open face and those guileless eyes, Adam knew he could not reveal his thoughts. Nor could he tell her that he was not a million miles away as she suggested, but very near their present location—in his bedchamber—and that she was there with him, beckoning him to make love to her. "I was thinking," he said, giving voice to the first thought that entered his head, "that I should like it if you called me by my name."

She stared at him, surprise written plainly upon her face. "What on earth prompted that idea?"

*What, indeed!*

Thinking fast, Adam said, "If we are to join forces to discover why Titus Brougham has come to Chelmford, we should do so as friends."

"Join forces? As friends?"

She blinked, and when her eyelashes touched her cheeks, the silky spikes glistened with a suspicious moisture. "Sir, I do not know what to say to your offer."

Adam stared at those damp eyelashes, unable to imagine what he had said to prompt them. Already he regretted having given voice to an utterly foolish idea; and yet, he had made the offer, and he would not go back on his word. "Say simply, 'I will do it, Adam.' "

"You are sincere? You will help me?"

"Word of a gentleman," he replied.

She smiled then, and Adam had the strangest feeling that the sun had finally penetrated the dense shade of the beech trees.

"Thank you," she said.

"Do not thank me yet, madam, for I have done nothing to deserve your gratitude."

"You offered to be my friend," she said, the words so soft, he almost did not hear them.

"As to that, half of London could tell you my friendship is not that much of a gift."

"It is to me, for I have never had a friend before."

"Never?"

She shook her head. "Not until today."

Adam returned to Jenson Hall still thinking about Marianne McCord. For his part, he did not believe she had anything to worry about as far as Titus Brougham was concerned. It was almost laughable to suspect that Brougham had come to Derbyshire with no other purpose than to lay claim to a house of no particular size or significance and an income of only two hundred pounds per annum.

Still, Adam had given his word that he would help

Marianne, and for that reason, as soon as he entered
the house, he went immediately to the large, high-ceil-
inged book room and composed a letter to his man of
business in London.

*Hildebrandt,*

*Be so good as to discover anything you can about
the recent activities of Mr. Titus Brougham. He has
come to Chelmford, and I wish to know if his reasons for doing so have anything to do with an estate
called Bibb Grange.*

*I shall expect to hear from you without delay.*

*Yr. Obd. Serv.*
*Jenson*

After sprinkling the vellum with sand so the ink
would not smudge, Adam thought of something else he
wanted to know.

*P.S. See if you can discover anything about a Lieu-
tenant Marcus Wilson, born about 1773. He was, for
a time, in Barbados.*

The postscript completed, Adam folded the letter and
sealed it with an unpretentious green wafer. He was
writing the direction of his man of business, when
someone knocked at the book-room door.

"Enter," he called. Expecting the intruder to be Sykes
or one of the footmen, Adam did not bother looking up
from his task.

"Well," said a familiar voice, "if this is all the greeting I can expect, perhaps I should return to town, where my presence is appreciated."

"Franklin!"

Tossing the stylus onto the desk, Adam stood and crossed the claret-colored carpet in six long strides, then grasped the hand of the one man in the world he would trust with his life. "I cannot think what has led you to believe that anyone in town appreciates your presence. However, I will admit that I am moderately happy to see you."

"Moderately! What a whisker, old fellow. Why, from the speed with which you crossed the room, I half expected you to fall on my neck and voice your undying gratitude to me for coming to save you from the boredom of country life."

After exchanging another round of insults, the two old friends retired to the upholstered wing chairs that flanked the fireplace, where they could partake of a glass of brandy and enjoy a comfortable coze. Naturally, Mr. Llewellyn asked after Adam's health. "Is the wound healing?"

"Yes, thank you." After a sip from his wineglass, Adam said, "I suppose the story of the duel is all over town."

Because his guest possessed the kind of open, honest face that would not allow him to tell a convincing lie, he did not reply to the remark. Instead, he smoothed his hand over the sleeve of the Prussian-blue coat that made the most of his very slender physique and his reddish-blond hair and blue eyes. "What think you of this new coat? I had it from Meyer, in Conduit Street, and though he is Prinny's favorite tailor, I am not certain the cut suits me."

Undeceived at his friend's attempt to turn the conversation, Adam said, "The talk is as bad as all that, is it?"

"Afraid so, old fellow."

Adam sighed. He had left town in the apparently misguided hope that without him there as a constant reminder, the scandal resulting from the duel would die a quick death. He had grown weary of the reputation that followed him—some of it deserved but most of it blown out of all proportion to the truth. Now all he wanted was to be left alone so he might rescue whatever honor still adhered to his name.

"And the wagers?" he asked.

"The Betting Book at White's is running two to one that you are the father of Lord Worley's heir, but I believe the wagers recorded at Brooks's favor a certain dark-haired member of Parliament who is famous for leaving his cuckoos in other men's nests."

Adam studied the amber liquid in his glass. "And what of Worley's accusation that I cheated at cards?"

"Deuce take it, Adam, I told you no one would believe that taradiddle. Everyone knows the duel was Worley's way of saving face over being a cuckold."

"You are certain?"

"Quite. Why, before he fled the country, the fool was bragging to anyone who would listen about how he had put a bullet in you. Of course, the real story was all over town—how he slipped in the mud, causing his weapon to discharge—so everyone was laughing at him behind his back."

"Poor Worley."

"Poor Worley! *Lucky* Worley, more like. Had you not deloped, he would now be occupying six feet of churchyard. Instead, he is aboard his yacht bound for the Greek islands."

His friend's wrath still roused, he continued. "And what of poor Jenson? The duel was not of your making, and yet it is you who received a bullet hole in your side. Incidentally, your man of business crossed a few palms with gold, so no charges were brought against you or Worley. By the time you are ready to return to town, I am persuaded the entire story will have been replaced by some other *on-dit.*"

"*If* I return to town."

"Do you think you might not?"

Adam shrugged. "Who is to say? I find I miss it less than I had expected, and the quiet of the country gives me time to reflect upon my past sins." *And,* he added to himself, *how I might make amends for one or two that were truly my doing.*

Nothing more was said of the duel, and the gentlemen sipped their brandy in companionable silence until Sykes scratched at the door to inform them that a cold collation was served. As they strolled across the corridor to the handsomely decorated dining room, Adam recalled his afternoon with Marianne McCord and his promise to help her. "By the way, Franklin, what do you know of Titus Brougham?"

"Very little," Mr. Llewellyn replied, "and none of it good."

It being the Sabbath, dinner at Bibb Grange was cold as well, with sandwiches and an almond-flavored trifle making up the entire meal. Not that Marianne noticed what she put into her mouth. Her mind was too occupied with recollections of her meeting in the wood with Adam Jenson.

What in heaven's name had possessed her to tell him the circumstances of her birth? In nearly twenty-six years, she had never told another living soul. So why had she shared this most intimate secret with a man who was practically a stranger to her? Say what he would about being her friend and wanting to help her, she had no reason to trust in his word or his ability to keep her secret to himself.

And yet, she did trust him. Without an ounce of justification for doing so, she trusted him.

She went to her bed that night still thinking of the warmth that had invaded her body when Adam Jenson had looked her over and the way she had imagined the feel of his lips on her skin. Within minutes, however, those thoughts were swept from her mind by the sound of thunder and the immediate noise of rain pounding the roof.

"Oh, no," she muttered, throwing back the covers and dashing across the room to the washstand, "not again."

She moved just in time, for as she placed the washbasin on the pillow where her head had lain only moments before, a large drop of water splattered on her outstretched arm. "Tarnation!" she said inelegantly. "First thing tomorrow I will go to the village and I will find someone to mend the roof. I will not take no for an answer, not even if I have to bring the thatcher here at gunpoint!"

The next morning, directly after she finished breaking her fast, Marianne made good her vow. While Georgie brought the trap around, Marianne asked Hannah where she should go. "I want a skilled workman."

"Vince Sims is the best thatcher, miss, but either one

of his sons will do a good job for you. That is, if they've free time."

Marianne knew this was Hannah's way of warning her that she might find the men unwilling to work for her, but she had to take that chance. God willing, she meant to live there for at least another fifty years, and there would always be things that wanted mending.

She followed Hannah's directions to the Sims cottage, but as it turned out, neither Sims nor his sons were at home. A toothless old woman answered the knock at the solid oak door, and upon spying Marianne, she said, "Sims b'aint here."

"And his sons?"

"They b'aint here neither."

"When will they return?" Marianne asked. "I am Miss McCord of Bibb Grange, and I need—"

"Know who you be."

Undeterred by the old woman's rudeness, Marianne continued. "I need the services of a good thatcher. I was told that Sims is the best, so—"

"B'aint home," she repeated. Apparently having said her piece, the toothless old crone stepped back and slammed the door.

Marianne starred at the solid oak structure as if she could see through it to the woman on the other side. If this reception was any indication, the villagers still meant to shun her.

More disappointed than angry and uncertain where to inquire next, Marianne returned to the trap. She had just lifted the ribbons to let Bess know it was time to plod on home, when she spied a horse and rider galloping down the lane. The rider was a woman, Marianne could tell that much at a distance, and from the looks of it, the lady had been born to the saddle.

Horse and rider moved in such harmony, they might almost have shared one brain, and as they drew near, Marianne watched them in admiration. They were a perfect combination, the young lady in her black habit atop a beautiful, graceful gray.

Marianne recognized the lady as Miss Havor, the tall blonde she had seen outside the church, the one who had been in conversation with Titus Brougham. As the rider galloped past her, Marianne raised her hand in greeting.

Miss Havor did not return her salute, but before Marianne knew what to think, the young lady had turned the gray and was coming back at a much slower pace. When she drew up next to the trap, she said, "Forgive me. I did not see you in time to return your wave."

"Think nothing of it, Miss Havor."

The young lady stared rather myopically, leading Marianne to suspect that the rider needed the aid of spectacles. "I am sorry," she said, "but have we met?"

"We have not. I saw you yesterday, outside the church, when you were conversing with Mr. Titus Brougham."

"You are a friend of Mr. Brougham's, then?"

Marianne shook her head. "We only just met. I am Marianne McCord, the new owner of Bibb Grange."

"Oh."

Miss Havor might need spectacles, but Marianne's eyesight was perfect, and she did not miss the look of indecision on the young lady's face. Fully expecting her to turn and gallop away, Marianne was pleased when Miss Havor remained. "I understand that you are new to Derbyshire," she said rather hesitantly. "I . . . I hope you like it."

"I should be hard to please if I did not. Indeed, I

cannot say enough about the beauty of the Peak District."

"You share my view on the subject, Miss McCord. And the grange? Do you think you will be happy there?"

"I already am. Or I will be once I find a thatcher. I cannot say I like jumping from my bed each time it rains to distribute pans about the place."

The young lady laughed, and the broad smile transformed her rather ordinary face into one that was quite charming. "It sounds most unpleasant."

"It is, and likely to be repeated. Vince Sims was from home, and I do not know where to go in search of another thatcher."

Miss Havor glanced back toward the cottage. "I believe I heard my father say he had seen the bailiff from Jenson Hall a day or so ago, and that the man mentioned the stables needed to be rethatched. I should not be at all surprised if Sims and both his sons are at the Hall."

Nothing more was said on the subject, for Miss Havor's groom had caught up with her, and both man and horse looked decidedly winded. "There you be, Miss Faye," the middle-aged servant said. "Fair give me the slip, you did."

"I am sorry, Jem."

"As well you should be, Miss Faye, for you know 'er ladyship will 'ave me 'ead on a platter if she finds out you've been riddin' neck or nothing again. 'Oydens don't get 'usbands, 'er ladyship'll say."

He touched his forelock to Marianne; then, in the style of servants who have known their charges since they were infants, he added, "Come along, now, Miss

Faye. Best not to keep the 'orses standing about in the wind."

Though not a breath of air stirred, the young lady did not argue. "You are right, of course."

With a smile of apology, she bid Marianne a polite farewell; then, though she did not appear to give the horse a signal of any kind, the gray turned and galloped away, leaving the groom and his mount behind.

"Miss Faye!" the servant yelled. "Wait up!" Muttering in exasperation, the servant urged his own horse forward, though it was obvious he would never catch up with his charge.

Marianne watched until both horses were out of sight, smiling to herself at Miss Havor's pluck. A hoyden she might be, and a bit tall into the bargain, but she was a pleasant young lady with a pretty smile, and Marianne doubted she would have any trouble finding a young man who would appreciate her finer qualities.

Encouraged by Miss Havor's friendly manner, Marianne made up her mind to find Sims and his sons. If necessary, she would offer them double the usual rate, for she could not allow the roof to continue to deteriorate.

Her resolve to see her house repaired kept her from crying craven while she drove the trap up the long, winding carriageway that led to Jenson Hall. She had all but forgotten the impressive limestone edifice with its extensive wings and the rectangular tower, and unlike the last time, when she had the injured viscount with her to ensure her a pleasant reception, this time she was alone. What if the bailiff took one look at her and threw her off the place?

Or what if Vince Sims told her in front of everyone that he would not work for her? Anything was possible.

Marianne had almost talked herself out of going all
the way to the stables, when she rounded a bend and
very nearly collided with a smart-looking maroon-and-
gold tilbury pulled by a high-stepping dun-colored
horse. To Marianne's dismay, the high-spirited animal
took immediate exception to Bess's occupancy of the
middle of the carriageway and reared up on its hind
legs, threatening to overturn the gig and spill the two
gentlemen occupants onto the ground.

The slender stranger who drove the gig was obliged
to employ all his strength to bring the horse under control, while the gentleman who sat beside him hung on
to the sides of the equipage, tainting the air with some
very ungentlemanly language.

"Madam!" Adam Jenson shouted once the dun was
finally brought to order. "What the devil are you doing
here? And why do you not shoot that four-legged men-
ace you call a horse before she gets you killed?"

# Six

"Sir, I am so sorry."

If Marianne hoped to calm the viscount, she was much mistaken. The moment he could do so, he leapt from the gig and came directly to her. "Are you injured?" he asked.

"No, I—"

"Damnation, Marianne, do the world a favor and tie a bell around that cow's neck. That way, the rest of us will have an even chance for survival."

Though they had only just avoided what might have proven a serious accident, the viscount's likening Bess to a cow struck Marianne as unbearably funny, and it was all she could do not to laugh. Keeping her lips from twitching was an impossibility, however, so she lifted her hand to her mouth to keep her angry neighbor from witnessing her amusement.

Unfortunately, the stratagem failed, and when the gentleman saw her smile, he grew incensed, caught her around the waist, and swung her down from the trap. "Make sport of me, will you?" he said, his arm still firmly circling her waist. "You should not, you know, for I have very effective ways of silencing laughter."

Their faces were mere inches apart, and Marianne could feel the warmth of his breath upon her forehead.

It was his eyes, though, that scorched her. Those dark orbs bore into hers, then his gaze slowly moved to her lips, sending shivers of anticipation down her spine. She knew he was about to kiss her, and she did nothing to prevent the assault.

"Marianne," he said, the word a mere whisper, then he dipped his head, displacing those inches that separated them. His mouth had almost touched hers, when the gentleman in the tilbury called out his name.

"Adam old fellow. Bad form to maul a lady about in a public lane. Well, it is your lane, of course, so it is private, but— Dash it all, Adam! Unhand her."

At his friend's admonition, Adam lifted his head again, leaving Marianne feeling as though she had been robbed. From the fire in Adam's eyes, he must have felt the same, and with his attention still upon her lips, he spoke to the gentleman in the tilbury. "And if I do not unhand her? What will you do, Franklin? Challenge me to a duel?"

"No, no. Of course not. Illegal now, don't you know. Nothing for it, old fellow, I shall be obliged to thrash you within an inch of your life."

At this, Adam burst out laughing and released Marianne, stepping back so she was free to do what she would. "Franklin, you idiot, when was the last time you got the better of me in fisticuffs?"

"Never, actually. But I am willing to see if this might be the time."

Marianne stepped around the viscount so she could speak to the much smaller gentleman who still sat on the gig's handsome gold leather seat. "Sir, you are very gallant, but I wish you will not do Lord Jenson bodily harm on my account."

"I will not, ma'am, if you should dislike it."

She heard Adam chuckle. "Trust me, Franklin, the lady would not dislike it nearly as much as you would."

Having said this, Adam touched Marianne's elbow and led her toward his friend.

"Miss McCord," he said, "allow me to present Mr. Franklin Llewellyn, my oldest friend."

"A pleasure, ma'am," the gentleman said, lifting his stylish beaver to reveal reddish-blond hair brushed back from a slender, yet attractive face.

"Mr. Llewellyn," she replied, curtsying. "The viscount told me not too many days ago that his friendship was not much of a gift. After witnessing his rubbishy treatment of you, I begin to believe the earlier assessment."

"Think nothing of it, Miss McCord, for I assure you I do not give it a thought. Adam and I met as boys at Harrow some twenty years ago, so I am accustomed to his manners. For the most part, I ignore his boorish behavior."

"You are very good, sir."

Adam cleared his throat, the gesture informing all who cared to know that he had grown weary of the discussion of himself. "When you two are finished vilifying me, perhaps Miss McCord would like to tell me why she was tooling up my carriageway. Did you wish to see me about something?"

"Not you, sir, but a workman who is thought to be at your stables. I hoped to bribe him into coming to the grange. During last evening's rain, I nearly drowned in my own bed, so today I went in search of a good thatcher. Miss Havor informed me that the man—"

"Miss Havor?" Mr. Llewellyn said. "Miss *Faye* Havor?"

"Why, yes. That is the young lady's name."

The gentleman assumed a not-too-convincing air of nonchalance. "Now you mention it, I believe I *do* remember hearing that she lived in Derbyshire. That is, if it is the same Miss Faye Havor. A blond lady?"

"Yes, she is a blond. With blue eyes and a pretty face."

"Oh," the gentleman said, "you think her pretty?"

"Who would not, after seeing her smile? And such style on horseback."

"Yes," Mr. Llewellyn said, an undisguised spark of pride in his eyes, "she is a gifted rider." He discovered a blemish on his tan kid driving gloves and studied the mark a moment. "You do not think her too tall?"

Marianne had no difficulty guessing the answer he wished to hear. "Too tall? Nonsense, sir. The young lady puts me in mind of a Grecian statue. One of the Graces, perhaps."

"Exactly," the gentleman said. "One of the Graces. You are very perceptive, Miss McCord."

"Very," Adam said.

The viscount had listened to this exchange with real interest, for to his knowledge, his friend had never before shown any particular interest in a marriageable female. Could it be that Franklin had come to Chelmford with something more in mind than visiting Jenson Hall? Answering his own question in the affirmative, Adam spared a moment to hope that the young lady was worthy of a man as fine as Franklin Llewellyn.

Thinking it was time he tabled Franklin's purpose in coming to the Hall and got back to his neighbor's reason for doing so, he recalled that she had said she hoped to "bribe" the workman into coming to the grange. Though she had spoken in jest, Adam knew that servants and artisans could be unbelievably stiff-rumped at imes. It crossed his mind that a woman who lived alone might have trouble getting workmen to come to her home.

"Return to the grange," he said, slipping his hand beneath her elbow and leading her back to the trap. "I will go to the stables and speak to the thatcher for you."

At the suggestion, she turned quite pink with embarrassment, confirming Adam's suspicion about the workmen. "Oh, no," she said. "I should speak to the thatcher myself."

"Go home," he repeated. "The man will be at your place tomorrow morning."

"But—"

"He will be there. I guarantee it."

Marianne felt her face burn knowing the workman might refuse to work for her, but there was little she could say to dissuade Adam from doing what he wished. After all, it was his property, and if he chose to tell her to go home, she had no alternative but to obey.

After a wave of farewell to Mr. Llewellyn, she turned Bess and began the trip back down the winding driveway and onto the lane. Upon reaching the grange, she left the mare in Georgie's capable hands and proceeded to the kitchen garden, where she found Hannah on her knees, a trowel in one hand and a clump of recently dug weeds in the other.

"Such a waste," Hannah said, tossing the clump into a bushel basket that was already filled to overflowing. "What were they thinking to let a perfectly good garden get into such a state?"

"It seems to be mostly weeds."

"It is that, miss, but I think I got to it in time to salvage a bed of shallots and some parsnips." She sat back on her heels and wiped her sleeve across her damp forehead. "Once the parsnips are dug, me and Georgie'll turn over the earth and let it lie fallow during the winter months. In the spring, I'll start planting for real, and come next June, you won't recognize this garden."

Marianne said all that was proper, congratulating Hannah on her industry, but silently she prayed they would still be at the grange next June. If Titus Brougham sued for possession of the property, she and Hannah both might be looking for a place to live.

After passing through the kitchen and entering the corridor that led to the front stairs, Marianne heard the echoing thud of the knocker at the entrance door. Not naive enough to expect a call from one of the ladies of the neighborhood, she opened the door slowly, not at all certain who might be outside.

Her worst fears were realized, for the man standing beneath the limestone arch was none other than Mr. Titus Brougham. Had she, by thinking of him, managed to conjure him up? She hoped not; otherwise, she would have to learn to guard her thoughts.

"Good afternoon," he said, smiling as if in no doubt of his welcome. "I hope I have not come at a bad time."

"Actually, sir, you have." Marianne did not open the door any wider but remained with her hand upon the jamb, her stance unwelcoming. "What is it you want, Mr. Brougham?"

He continued to smile as if she had been the soul of cordiality. "My purpose in coming here is no great mystery, Miss McCord, and I shall be more than happy to reveal it to you. May I come in?"

"Forgive me, sir, but I am not ready to receive guests."

"I scarcely qualify as a guest, dear lady. After all, I am one of the family."

"Of the Bibb family, perhaps. You are not, however, a member of *my* family. Furthermore, you must know that as a woman alone, I cannot entertain a gentleman without the chaperonage of another female."

He put his hand upon the door, giving it just the least little push. "Really, Miss McCord, must we stand on ceremony? I grew weary of the limited society at the Swan, and I meant only to take a sentimental journey through a house I once visited as a young man. What harm can there be in that?"

Somehow, that slight push on the door convinced Marianne that there might be harm in abundance if she allowed Titus Brougham inside the house. Standing her ground, she said, "Again, sir, you must forgive me, but I cannot allow you to come inside."

"But, my dear young lady, you cannot refuse me a visit in a house that is, in truth, more mine than yours?"

"I can, and I do. Good day, Mr. Brougham."

Having said all that was necessary, Marianne slowly shut the door. To her relief, the man did not attempt to stop her, and once the door was closed and the bolt shot, she turned and ran up the stairs, not stopping until she reached the relative security of her bedchamber.

Mr. Brougham's rather spurious story about wishing to take a walk down memory lane was just that, a story, and Marianne did not believe it for an instant. As for his thinly veiled allegation that the house should have been his, that made her feel more uneasy than she would like to admit.

Determined to do now what she should have done the previous day, the minute she returned from church,

Marianne went straight to the Queen Anne desk and took a seat in the splat-back chair. After removing a sheet of vellum from the small stack that reposed on the corner of the smooth walnut surface, she pulled forward a pewter tray bearing a plain crockery ink pot and a pair of styluses. Marianne lifted the cap of the ink pot, dipped the nib into the dark liquid, then began a letter to Mr. Penell, Theodore Bibb's solicitor, asking him to send her a true and unabridged copy of Mr. Bibb's last will and testament.

"The will," she said, penning the solicitor's direction in the Inns of Court in London, "should tell me where I stand. It may even give some indication of how I am to thwart Titus Brougham in his bid to gain Bibb Grange. As thwart him I will."

Whatever the old gentleman's reasons, Theodore Bibb had meant Daisy McCord to have Bibb Grange, and Marianne was not giving it up without a fight!

In search of a wafer, Marianne tried once again to open the shallow drawer in the desk. As before, it would not budge. Something was definitely holding it shut. After reminding herself to bring up a long knife to see if she could force the drawer open, she went belowstairs to the kitchen to employ a bit of paraffin to seal the letter.

The evening was quiet enough, with Marianne and Hannah sitting at the small oak worktable in the housekeeper's room, applying needle and thread to a stack of linen that wanted mending. Georgie had lain on the floor, playing with the three kittens, until he and the felines had grown tired and sought their beds. Not ten minutes later, Hannah yawned and stretched, hinting at her own wish to get some much-needed sleep.

With everyone else abed, Marianne took her work candle and lit her way to her own chamber, where she lay awake for some time, her mind filled with the events of the day, not the least of which was her meeting with Miss Havor and her introduction to Adam's friend, Mr. Llewellyn.

Having saved the best memory for last, Marianne was reliving the kiss Adam Jenson had almost given her, when she was snatched from that pleasurable reminiscence by the sound of something crashing to the floor in the blue-and-white parlor. Because that room was directly below her bedchamber, there was no mistaking the direction of the sound.

Something had fallen, and Marianne was human enough to wish that someone else—anyone but her—would investigate. Hannah and Georgie were below-stairs, of course, but their rooms were at the back of the house, off the kitchen, and they had gone to bed hours earlier. That left only Marianne.

After relighting the candle on her bedside table, she armed herself with the iron poker from the fireplace, then she opened her bedchamber door and made her way rather slowly down the stairs. If an intruder were in the parlor, she had no wish to confront him, so with each step she said a silent prayer that any malefactors would see her light and run away.

The intruder—if such a person truly existed—did not run toward the vestibule to escape through the front door, but that fact did not reassure Marianne to any great degree. Feeling anything but confident, she paused to take a deep breath, raised the poker so she might use it if need be, then stepped just inside the parlor.

There was no one to be seen. Feeling a bit braver,

she held the candle aloft and scanned the four corners of the room. The parlor was empty.

As the faint pool of candlelight fell upon the inglenook, the yellow-striped mother cat whom Georgie had named Butterball crawled from beneath one of the upholstered benches, a now-lifeless mouse dangling from her mouth.

Marianne breathed a sigh of relief. "Thank heaven," she said, "the intruder has four legs."

It was not clear whether she referred to the cat or the mouse, but Butterball gave Marianne a look that labeled *her* the intruder. With the air of a mighty hunter, the cat sauntered past the human and exited the room, taking her prize with her. Within moments she had disappeared down the dark corridor, her destination the kitchen.

"What a fool I am," Marianne said, lowering the poker. She had wanted a mouser, and now she had one. "And a good one apparently."

Feeling like the veriest ninnyhammer, Marianne vowed she would not become one of those crazy old spinsters who jumped at every sound and who could not go to sleep without first checking beneath her bed. Grateful that she had not roused Hannah from her sleep to witness such cork-brained behavior, Marianne turned to retrace her steps to her bedchamber. As she passed the rosewood worktable, something caught her attention.

On the floor beside the table lay a broken lamp, the pieces of the etched glass shade strewn all about, but it was not the sight of the shattered lampshade that made Marianne's knees quake as though she had seen a ghost. After all, common sense told her that Butterball might have knocked over the lamp. What caused

Marianne's legs to tremble and her stomach muscles to tighten into a painful knot was the sight of the small ledger in which she recorded all her expenditures.

The ledger lay facedown on the worktable, the pages crumpled as though the book had been put down quickly. And yet, Marianne recalled quite distinctly having returned the book to its usual place on the middle shelf of the vitrine.

Knowing full well that Hannah would never read anything as personal as an accounts ledger, never mind leave it lying about, Marianne felt her earlier fear return. Only this time she *knew* someone had been in the house. At least, she hoped the incident was in the past tense!

Not willing to find out, she turned and ran from the room, and as she sped up the stairs to the next floor, her bare feet barely touched the treads. Like one pursued, she did not stop for anything until she reached the safety of her bedchamber; then, after turning the key in the lock, she wedged a chair beneath the doorknob for good measure. Though she snuck a quick peek beneath her bed, Marianne did not blow out her candle, nor did she close her eyes until the morning sun sent shafts of light to dispel the darkness.

# Seven

The sound of voices outside her window roused Marianne rather early, and though she had slept for perhaps no more than two hours, she came awake quickly, threw back the covers, and went to the window to see what was happening.

"Bring it over 'ere, Ben," said a stockily built man in his mid-fifties who stood in the carriageway.

Dressed in a workman's smock and a slouched felt hat, he shouted instructions to a second man, who was about Hannah's age but similarly dressed and equally hearty-looking. The younger man drove a two-wheeled cart loaded to overflowing with fresh yellow straw, and though the straw might have been intended for a number of uses, the tools tied to the sides of the cart were unmistakably those of the thatcher's trade.

There was a rake made of a stout ash rod with large nails at the end to form the teeth, a flat knife mounted on a handle like a trowel, a reaping hook, shears, and a two-part wooden ladder. The tools were no different from those used by thatchers centuries earlier, but even though they appeared primitive, Marianne knew that in the hands of an experienced artisan, the old-fashioned implements were as effective as the latest inventions.

"We'll start at this corner," said the man she assumed was Vince Sims.

The younger man, presumably Sims's son, drove the cart quite close to the house, then he yelled, "Way," to halt the pony. As soon as the animal stopped, the driver jumped to the ground and began unlashing the tools and laying them across a pair of sawhorses, where they were easily accessible. While he wound the securing rope around his arm and placed it on the seat of the cart, his father removed the two parts of the ladder and began fitting them together into one, making it long enough to reach up to the second-story roof.

As Vince and Ben Sims went about their business, Marianne closed her eyes for a moment, grateful to know that Adam had kept his word to send the workmen and thankful that with the coming of the thatchers, at least one of her problems would soon be solved.

But what of her other worries? What of Titus Brougham and his possible wish to have Bibb Grange for himself? And what of the mysterious intruder?

Marianne was still disturbed by what had happened the night before. Though in the clear light of day, what bothered her even more than the discovery that someone had, indeed, been inside the house, was the revelation that she was not as brave as she had always fancied herself to be. Not that she had ever been in that particular situation before; still, she did not like having to admit that she had behaved like a scared rabbit.

It was bad enough to be frightened by the presence of some unknown person. It was much worse, however, to allow fear to get so far out of hand that it made one a victim twice over.

Marianne's unproductive self-recriminations were interrupted by a knock at her bedchamber door. Thinking it must be Hannah, Marianne was about to call "Enter," when she realized the door was still locked. Not wanting anyone else to know of her cowardice, she hurried across the room, removed the chair from beneath the knob, then turned the key in the lock. To her surprise, Georgie greeted her with a smile.

In his hands he carried an ordinary earthenware jug wrapped in a kitchen cloth, but Marianne was not deceived into believing the excitement in his blue eyes had anything to do with the rather mundane task of supplying her with hot water.

"The thatchers be here, miss."

"I am happy to know it. As, I see, are you."

The boy nodded. "Mama said I could go out and watch 'em work soon as I brought up your gugglet."

"My what?"

"Gugglet, miss." Georgie glanced toward the jug he still held. "On account of it goes *guggle, guggle* when you pour the water."

Yielding to such indisputable logic, Marianne instructed him to set the gugglet on the washstand. "And thank you, Georgie, for bringing it up."

The boy did as he was bid, but almost before she had finished thanking him, he had dashed out the door and was running down the stairs, eager to be outside, watching the thatchers. From the loud *thump, thump* against the side of the house, the workmen were at that moment positioning the long ladder before climbing up to the sharply slanted rooftop, and if Marianne was any judge of the matter, such a climb was a feat of derring-do no young boy would want to miss.

As for Marianne, there was excitement enough for her in knowing she would no longer be obliged to set out pans to catch the leaks each time it rained. Certain

## We'd Like to Invite You to Subscribe t[ ]
## Zebra's Regency Romance Book Club a[ ]
## Give You a Gift of 4 Free Books as You[ ]
## Introduction! (Worth $19.96!)

If you're a Regency lover, imagine the joy of getting **4 FR[ ]
Zebra Regency Romances** and then the chance to have t[ ]
lovely stories delivered to your home each month at the
lowest prices available! Well, that's our offer to you and
here's how you benefit by becoming a Regency Romance
subscriber:

- **4 FREE Introductory Regency Romances are delivered to your doo[ ]**

- **4 BRAND NEW Regencies are then delivered each month (usually be[ ]
  they're available in bookstores)**

- **Subscribers save almost $4.00 every month**

- **Home delivery is always FREE**

- **You also receive a FREE monthly newsletter, *Zebra/Pinnacle Rom[ ]
  News* which features author profiles, contests, subscriber benefits, [ ]
  previews and more**

- **No risks or obligations...in other words you can cancel whenever y[ ]
  wish with no questions asked**

Join the thousands of readers who enjoy the savings and
convenience offered to Regency Romance subscribers. Afte[ ]
your initial introductory shipment, you receive 4 brand-new
Zebra Regency Romances each month to examine for 10 da[ ]
Then, if you decide to keep the books, you'll pay the preferr[ ]
subscriber's price of just $4.00 per title. That's only $16.00 f[ ]
all 4 books and there's never an extra charge for shipping
and handling.

### It's a no-lose proposition, so return the
### FREE BOOK CERTIFICATE today!

## Say Yes to 4 Free Books!
### Complete and return the order card to receive this
### $19.96 value, ABSOLUTELY FREE!

If the certificate is missing below, write to:
Zebra Home Subscription Service, Inc.,
P.O. Box 5214, Clifton, New Jersey 07015-5214
or call TOLL-FREE 1-888-345-BOOK

Visit our website at www.kensingtonbooks.com.

## FREE BOOK CERTIFICATE

**YES!** Please rush me 4 Zebra Regency Romances without cost or obligation. I understand that each month thereafter I will be able to preview 4 brand-new Regency Romances FREE for 10 days. Then, if I should decide to keep them, I will pay the money-saving preferred subscriber's price of just $16.00 for all 4...that's a savings of almost $4 off the publisher's price with no additional charge for shipping and handling. I may return any shipment within 10 days and owe nothing, and I may cancel this subscription at any time. My 4 FREE books will be mine to keep in any case.

Name _____

Address _____ Apt. _____

City _____ State _____ Zip _____

Telephone ( ) _____

Signature _____
(If under 18, parent or guardian must sign.)

RN050A

Terms and prices subject to change. Orders subject to acceptance by Zebra Home Subscription Service, Inc. Offer valid in U.S. only.

lll..l..l.lll...l..lll.l.l.l..l.ll.l..l.l..ll.l..ll.l.l..l

**REGENCY ROMANCE BOOK CLUB**
Zebra Home Subscription Service, Inc.
P.O. Box 5214
Clifton NJ 07015-5214

PLACE STAMP HERE

she would never get back to sleep, she poured the steaming water into the washbasin, removed her plain white night rail, then took her time over her ablutions, all the while remembering the moment when she had discovered that someone had been in the blue-and-white parlor.

Not yet decided if she should tell Hannah about the incident, Marianne had just stepped into a faded brown frock she had worn many times these past five years, when she heard hoofbeats on the hard-packed earth of the carriageway.

"Your lordship!" Georgie called in greeting. "I didn't know you were coming over as well. Look," he added as if offering a rare treat, "the thatchers are come to fix our roof."

"So I see," Adam Jenson replied. "Are you to be their new helper?"

"No, sir. But Ben says I'm allowed to watch them all I want, so long as I don't get too close to the house. The pitch of our roof is really steep, and Ben says sometimes when his hands get sweaty, he'll accidentally drop a tool. I'm to keep my distance so I don't get hit by anything he might drop."

"Sounds good advice, lad, and I think I will follow your example. Before I do anything else, though, I must find someplace safe to tie my horse."

*Tie his horse!*

When Marianne first heard Adam's voice, she had paused in her dressing, undecided what to do. But now that she knew he meant to stay long enough to warrant dismounting and securing his horse, she knew exactly what course to follow. After allowing the brown frock to fall to the floor, she kicked it aside, then rummaged in the clothespress until she found her yellow sprigged muslin.

The dress was far from new, but her looking glass told her the simple lines were flattering to her figure, while the deep golden yellow of the tiny flowers brought out the green in her eyes. After donning the muslin, Marianne grabbed a chip straw Gypsy hat to protect her face from the morning sun; then, after tying the wide ribbons beneath her chin, she hurried down the stairs and out the front door.

At the top of the three shallow steps, she paused, feigning surprise. "Why, Lord Jenson. How do you do, sir? Did you ride over to see that the workmen had fulfilled your promise to me?"

"Not at all," he replied. "I came to see you." After giving her a quick perusal that did not miss an inch of her, he added, "And I have been amply rewarded for my efforts."

Though Marianne knew she should tell him in no uncertain terms that he was not to pay her compliments, she could not hide the smile that sprang to her lips at his approval of her appearance. "Lord Jenson," she said, "you . . . you pass the line of what is pleasing."

"Liar."

"Sir!"

Adam placed his booted foot on the bottom step and leaned forward so that he and she were close enough not to be overheard. "Like all beautiful women," he said, "you appreciate an occasional reminder that your beauty has not gone unnoticed."

Marianne's heart picked up its pace, but she was not certain if the cause was the gentleman's words or his nearness. "I am not like other beautiful women." Aghast at what she had said, she hurried to amend her statement. "What I meant to say was that I am *not* beautiful."

"Why, madam," he said as if shocked, "are you fishing for more compliments?"

"Of course not! How could you even think—." She paused, for she had spied the spark of light in his dark eyes, and she knew he was roasting her. "Adam Jenson, are there no limits to your wickedness? How far will you go to hear me cry 'uncle'?"

"Pansy eyes," he said, the words low and soft, like a caress, "you must know it is not 'uncle' I wish to hear you cry out. It is 'Adam.' "

"Sir! I did not say cry *out,* and well you know it."

"My mistake," he said, raising an eyebrow in that mocking manner that quite stole Marianne's breath away. "At least" he added, "you did not go all missish and pretend not to understand me."

Warmth stole up Marianne's neck to invade her face, for she realized too late that she should have feigned ignorance of his veiled allusion to a cry heard in the heat of passion. Before she could think what to say, however, he caught her hand and lifted it to his lips, the gesture one of apology.

"Forgive me," he said, "but I could not resist teasing you a bit. Did I not warn you that I was unfit company for a gently reared young lady?"

Marianne searched within her for the indignation a real lady would feel at such unseemly behavior from a gentleman, but she could not find it. All she discovered was a knee-weakening desire to feel Adam Jenson's lips upon her mouth as they had been upon her hand.

Afraid that he would read her wanton thoughts, she turned her head slightly, allowing the wide brim of the

Gypsy hat to hide her face from view. "You said you came to see me, my lord. May I ask why? Assuming, of course, that this continued foolishness has not caused you to forget your purpose."

He laughed aloud. "I have not forgotten, madam. Nor am I fooled by your attempt to hide behind that rather fetching bonnet."

Reminded of her cowardice the previous evening when she hid in her bedchamber, Marianne turned away completely.

Adam watched her turn. He had no idea what he had said, but he knew immediately that something was not right. One minute his lovely neighbor had been holding her own in their banter, with her head high and her eyes bright with enjoyment, and the next minute she showed him her back, her head all but bowed.

"Marianne? What is amiss?"

"Nothing."

Adam had been lied to by experts, and this novice did not even know how to begin to dissemble. "Tell me," he said.

This time she merely shook her head. If she thought to evade him, however, she mistook her man. Resolved to know what was troubling her, he stepped up beside her, took her by the shoulders, and turned her around to face him. "If you were any other young lady, I would ask if I had said something to offend you, then I would beg your pardon. Thankfully, you are not one of those young ladies. You are refreshingly honest and blessedly forthright, and if I had offended you, you would have rung a peal over me and had done with it.

"That said, I ask you again, madam, what is amiss?"

She looked up at him then, distress in her eyes but

resolve in the firmness of her chin. "I am a coward, Adam."

"Never!"

"It is true." The words seemed almost to choke her, and she was obliged to swallow before she continued. "Last night I—"

"Wait." Adam held up his hand for silence. He knew for a fact that young Georgie was within hearing distance, and standing as they were, just beneath the stone arch of the doorway, Adam could not be certain their conversation was not providing a month's worth of gossip for the two men on the roof. "We cannot talk here," he said. "Come, let us walk toward the lane."

When she offered no resistance, he placed her hand in the crook of his arm and led her down the carriageway, almost to the drystone wall. At the entrance to the property, they stopped beside a patch of dark pink ragged robin, where an iron gate lay on the ground, rusted and forgotten.

"Now," Adam said, "tell me about last night."

She made short work of the story, faltering only once, and that was when she told him how she had dashed up the stairs, locked her door, then sat up most of the night, frightened out of her wits.

"As you had every right to be," he said. "Now tell me the part you believe brands you a coward."

The lady's face turned a bright pink. "That was it."

"That?"

When she nodded, he said, "Let me see if I have the particulars in proper order. You hear a noise, you investigate, you discover unquestionable proof that someone is in your house, then you run to the safety of your room and lock yourself inside. If this is cowardice, I applaud it."

When she drew breath as if to argue, Adam continued. "Had you a loaded pistol with which to defend yourself?"

"No, of course not. As far as I know, there is not a pistol in the house."

"What of fisticuffs? Are you, perhaps, handy with your fives?"

"With my fives? What on earth—"

"Wrestling, then? Do you practice the ancient sport of Greco-Roman wrestling?"

From the stubborn set of her chin, the lady was growing weary of his questions. "Adam, you are being foolish."

"Am I?"

"Of course you are."

He shook his head. "I think not. What would have been foolish is for a young woman of no more than eight stone to confront who-knows-how-large a man who had broken into her house. Had you forced his hand, the fellow might have done you serious physical injury. And had you chosen to scream for help, he might have visited a similar punishment upon the only other two people in the house. I presume you would not have wanted Georgie or his mother to suffer on your account."

"You know I would not."

"That being true, I am persuaded you chose the only sane course of action."

When she tipped her head, hiding once again behind the brim of that blasted hat, Adam put his hand beneath her chin and forced her to look up at him. As he had suspected, her eyes glistened with unshed tears, and he was about to take her in his arms to offer her the comfort she needed, when young Georgie came running down the carriageway, yelling at the top of his lungs.

"Your lordship!" he yelled. "Help! It's the thatchers."

Adam stepped away from Marianne and turned toward the boy who had only just reached them. Georgie's breath was coming in gasps, and he held his side with one hand; with the other he pointed back toward the house.

Marianne knew that Georgie would never call attention to himself if something quite serious had not occurred, and when she looked where the lad pointed, her worst fears were confirmed. What she saw put all else from her mind, for Vince Sims was balanced on the very top of the roof, where the two slopes met. While he held to one of the brick chimneys with one hand, he stared helplessly at his son, who appeared to be sitting atop one of the attic dormers a good ten feet below.

"Ben's caught," Georgie managed to say between gulps of air. "The place where the two ladders are joined gave way, and the ladders began to come undone. To save himself a fall"—the boy drew a deep breath— "Ben jumped onto the dormer. When he landed, his leg went through the roof, and now he's caught fast, unable to move."

Now Marianne understood why the man appeared to be sitting on the dormer. His entire leg must have gone through a weak spot in the old thatch, and without the ladder, which lay broken into pieces on the ground two stories below, his father could not get down to help pull him free. Both men were in danger, for should Vince Sims lose his footing, there was nothing to stop him from experiencing the same fate as the ladder. Even if such a fall did not prove fatal, it was certain to leave the man with broken bones.

Though Marianne had not the first idea how she could be of assistance, she began to run toward the house. To her relief, Adam soon passed her by, his long, powerful legs taking him down the carriageway in a matter of seconds. While he ran, he stripped off his snug-fitting coat and waistcoat and flung them aside, not caring that they landed in the dirt.

By the time Marianne reached the house, Adam had climbed up the limestone arch above the entrance door. Once he was balanced on the arch, he caught hold of the sill of one of the windows of the master bedchamber and began pulling himself up. Marianne held her breath, afraid his foot might slip or the sill might give way in his hand, causing him to fall. The very idea that Adam could be injured made Marianne's heart pound painfully in her chest.

Fortunately, he was quite strong, and though his progress was slow, he had no difficulty hoisting himself into a standing position at the window. As Marianne watched Adam attempt to find a toehold in the brick so he could climb even higher, all the way up to the dormer, she said a prayer for his safety. If only the ladder was still usable. Or if he had one of those picks rock climbers used. And a good rope!

At that last thought, Marianne recalled the ropes the thatcher had used to secure his tools to the farm cart. When he had unlashed the tools, he had wound the lengths of hemp, then placed them on the seat of the cart. Happy to have thought of something that might aid Adam—and the thatchers too, of course—Marianne ran to the cart.

It was the work of a moment to grab the ropes then

run into the house and up the stairs to her bedchamber. At first, Adam was nowhere to be seen, but when Marianne opened the window and leaned out, she saw him just above her. He had already reached the roof and was leaning against it, his chest flat against the thatching and his arms spread wide, using whatever handhold he could find. Moving slowly, he inched toward the dormer and young Sims.

"Adam," Marianne called softly. "Can you hear me?"

"I hear you," he said, his voice sounding strained and oddly muffled by the layers of compressed straw only inches from his face.

"I have two ropes," she said. "From the cart."

"Good girl! That is just what we need. Though how you are to get them to me, I confess I do not know."

"The dormer," she said. "I will hand them to you through the dormer."

Without waiting to hear any alternative plans he might have, Marianne ran from her bedchamber, hurried up the narrow wooden stairs that led to the two attic rooms, and flung open the door. She thanked heaven that she and Hannah had been so meticulous in their cleaning of the attic, for the few items that remained stored there were stacked neatly against the wall, offering no hindrance in her dash to the window.

There was, however, one obstacle in her path, and that was a man's long leg. It protruded through the roof, dangling from the ceiling like some nightmarish chandelier. As Marianne approached the leg, careful not to touch it, she noted that Ben's boot was still on his foot, though his breeches had been ripped apart at the seams, revealing a deep gash that ran from his knee all the way up his thigh. To Marianne's horror, the gash was spilling an unbelievable amount of blood.

Avoiding the leg and the dark red puddle on the thatch-strewn floor beneath it, Marianne reached the dormer, released the hatch, and pulled the small casement window toward her. Immediately, fresh air filled the room.

"Adam?"

"I am here," he replied, the words softly spoken.

Alarmed by the quiet reply, Marianne grasped the rope firmly in her hand, then shoved her arm out the window as far as possible. "I am just beneath the thatcher, Adam, and I can see his leg. It came all the way through the roof."

She heard the injured man clear his throat. "Beggin' your pardon, miss, but 'ow does it look? It 'urts sommit fierce."

"I do not doubt it, for there is a rather nasty cut and it is bleeding. As far as I can tell, however, there are no broken bones."

The thatcher exhaled rather loudly. "Thank you, miss."

Knowing she could do nothing at the moment to ease the workman's pain, she returned her attention to the viscount. "I am holding the rope out toward you, Adam. Can you see it? If so, tell me which way to move. Left? Right? Up? Down? Just give me directions, and I will follow them to the letter."

"I see the rope," he said. "Unfortunately, directions will not help."

She knew it! Somehow she had known something was not right. "What is amiss? The truth, Adam."

"The truth," he said, "is that the thatch between where I stand and the dormer is far too thin to bear my weight, leaving me with no way to get closer to Ben or to the rope."

Fear made Marianne's lips tremble. "What will you do now?"

"There is nothing I can do," he replied. "Not without experiencing a similar fate as the thatcher. Or worse."

# Eight

*Or worse.*

Those words struck fear in Marianne's heart, and for several moments she fought the feeling of helplessness that threatened to overcome her. After those first moments, however, she chided herself for wasting precious time. Three men were stranded on her roof, and if they were to have even a chance at escaping injury, they needed the ropes she held.

"Adam?" she called again. "I have a plan. It might not work, and you will probably think me a fool for suggesting it, but—"

"Modesty be damned!" he said. "If you have a plan, let us hear it. Believe me, the workmen and I are hanging on your every word."

"Very well," she said. "If I can fit through the casement window, how far will I have to crawl out to pass the rope to either you or Ben?"

Adam did not answer her right away, and Marianne thought he meant to ignore her question. In this, she was mistaken, for he had merely been considering his answer.

"Ben?"

"Yes, my lord?"

"I can expect no help from the gods, for I have offended them beyond redemption, but if you have not, we may just have a chance to get out of this nasty predicament. What say you? If Miss McCord somehow manages to squeeze through that very small window and perches on the sill, do you think you could reach down and take the rope from her?"

Marianne heard movement on the dormer roof just above her head, and at the same time, the workman's injured leg shifted position slightly. The movement was accompanied by a gasp of pain, then, "I believe I can reach the rope, my lord."

"Good man."

Though Adam kept a positive note in his voice, Marianne could hear an underlying fatigue creeping in. Knowing it must be costing him dearly to remain as he was, pressed against the steeply slanted roof, she hurried across the room to the far wall, where she and Hannah had dragged a large leather-covered seaman's chest. Fear for Adam's safety augmented Marianne's usual strength, and she caught the handle, tugged at the heavy chest until it began to move, then dragged it over to the window and shoved it against the wall.

Somewhere along the way she had lost her chip straw Gypsy hat, so all she had to contend with was the gently flowing skirt of her yellow sprigged muslin. She had just gathered the skirt in her hand and climbed up on the seaman's chest, when Adam called to her again.

"Marianne?"

"Yes?"

"Tie one of the ropes around your waist, then secure it to something in the room. No point in all four of us becoming stranded."

At the thought, Marianne was obliged to swallow a large obstruction in her throat. She had no head for heights, and she prayed she would not disgrace herself. Forcing her fear aside, she obeyed Adam's instructions by tying one end of the shorter rope around her waist, then looping the other end through the handles of the seaman's chest.

"Done," she called out.

"Excellent. Now listen carefully. Once you have handed off the second rope to Ben, do not release your end of it immediately. Instead, I want you to return to the attic, remove the rope from your waist, then tie the first rope to the second. Ben will then pull them both up. We may have need of their combined lengths."

Marianne nodded, then realizing that Adam could not see her, she said, "I will do as you say."

After stepping up onto the seaman's chest, she raised her arms over her head, bent forward, then began to ease herself through the small square opening. It was a tight squeeze, but by freeing first one shoulder, and then the other, she finally succeeded in working her upper torso through the casement window. Unfortunately, her lower torso was a different matter altogether.

She moaned. She groaned. She pushed. She pulled. She held her breath. She blew it out. Nothing she tried seemed to work. Though her hips were not particularly broad, their feminine roundness exceeded the width of the window.

After a time, with her skin slick from perspiration and her arms and hands stinging from numerous small scrapes and cuts, Marianne admitted defeat. Biting back the tears, she said, "I cannot get through. I am so sorry. If I weighed a stone less, perhaps—"

"I can do it!" said an excited boyish voice from somewhere inside the attic room. "I can get through the window, miss."

"Georgie?"

"Yes, miss."

Though Marianne attempted to look into the room, she found it impossible to do so, wedged as she was in the embrasure. "Is your mother there, Georgie?"

"I'm here too, miss," Hannah replied. "What can I do for you?"

"For one thing, you can pull me free of this trap. I got myself in here, but without assistance I doubt I can get out."

Hannah and Georgie each took one of Marianne's ankles, and pulling with all their strength, mother and son tugged her from the window. Thankfully, they curtailed their enthusiasm just before Marianne's head and arms slipped through the casement frame, thereby saving her from the pain of landing on the hard seaman's chest and cracking her skull.

As she sat up, Marianne swiped the back of her hand across her face, banishing the tears that spilled onto her cheeks. "I thought I could make it. Now what is Adam—are the men to do?"

"I can get through," Georgie said once again. "I'm small for my age."

"And very brave," Marianne said. "But . . ." She looked at Hannah, whose blue eyes had grown wide with apprehension.

"Oh, no," Hannah said. "He's just a boy, and much too small to—"

"That is just the point," Marianne said softly. "He is small enough to get through where I could not. He need only stand up on the windowsill and pass the rope up to Ben."

Hannah's face turned ashen. "But what if he should fall? He's—"

"I won't fall, Mama. I'll be real careful."

"He will not fall," Marianne said. "We can tie the second rope around Georgie's waist, just as I tied it around mine, and you and I will each hold one of his feet."

While Hannah considered the possibility of allowing her only child to climb out a second-story window, some of the rotten thatch around Ben Sims's trapped leg gave way, and the workman sunk farther into his snare, his foot almost touching Georgie's head.

"Aaee!" Ben cried out.

Unable to ignore the cry of pain, and the ever-growing pool of blood, Hannah nodded her consent. "Georgie can do it," she said, "but it's me what'll tie the knot."

"Of course," Marianne replied. "Whatever you say."

Though Georgie was too excited to stand still, his mother managed to tie the rope about his waist to her satisfaction. When she finally gave him her permission to go, the boy scooted through the window as fast as a sand lizard darts across the banks of a brook. Once the lad was standing upright on the sill, with Hannah and Marianne gripping his ankles tight enough to threaten their future circulation, Ben Sims leaned down from the dormer roof and snatched the second rope from Georgie's hands.

"Much obleeged, youngster."

When both ropes were finally in their possession, the three men made short work of getting off the grange roof. Once Vince Sims caught the coils his son tossed, he secured the end of the hemp around the nearest chimney, wound several lengths around his strong arm—from elbow to palm—then he tossed the free end to Adam. With the aid of the rope, Adam eased his way across the worn roof to the dormer.

Though Ben had lost a lot of blood, he was able to help Adam lift him up and out of the break in the roof. He cried out only once, then bit his lip to keep from doing so again.

"Sorry, old fellow," Adam said.

"Never mind me, sir. I'm that grateful to your lordship for coming to fetch me."

While Ben rested against the side of the dormer to catch his breath, Adam wrapped the rope around the injured man's waist, then he removed his handkerchief and tied the linen around the deep gash in Ben's thigh.

"Perhaps that will inhibit the flow a bit until we can get that little scratch stitched up."

"Thank you, sir."

"Do not thank me yet. Regrettably, the rope is not long enough to allow your father and me to lower you to the ground, so I propose we deposit you through that bedchamber window directly below here. What say you? Do you think you can make it?"

"I'll make it, sir."

Adam gave the knotted rope one last check. "I shall be as careful as possible guiding you down, but I warn you, it may prove a bumpy ride."

"I'm ready, my lord."

"Marianne," Adam called. "Ben will need help coming through that bedchamber window."

"We will be there," she yelled back.

While Adam helped Ben slip over the edge of the roof, and Vince Sims slowly unwound the lengths of rope from around his arm, easing his son's descent, the women and Georgie ran down the narrow attic stairs and into the master bedchamber.

Within less than two minutes, Marianne and Hannah had caught hold of Ben's good leg and were hauling him in through the large window.

"Steady there," Marianne said. "We'll try not to hurt you any more than necessary."

They did hurt him, of course, for they had to lift his injured leg over the sill, but Ben bore their handling without a whimper, the only sound his sigh of relief when his good foot finally touched the bedchamber floor.

While Marianne untied the rope, Hannah slipped her arm around the thatcher's ribs. "Here," she said, catching his right arm and draping it over her shoulder, "lean on me."

He did as she suggested. In fact, he wrapped his left arm around her shoulders as well, for all the world as if he had forgotten about the pain in his injured leg. "Much obleeged, Miss Scott."

"Why, Ben Sims," she said, "we've known each other since we were both no bigger than tadpoles. When did you start talking so formal like?"

"Just now," he said, "when I got a whiff of 'ow good them pretty red curls smell up close."

Marianne thought she had seen Hannah blush before, but nothing had prepared her for the degree of color that stole up her housekeeper's neck at the thatcher's slightly flirtatious compliment.

"Behave yourself, Ben Sims! A fine way to talk while

standing here in Miss McCord's bedchamber, dripping blood all over her carpet. When it's thanking her you should be for aiding in your rescue."

Ben Sims ducked his head like a chastened boy. "Beggin' your pardon, Miss McCord. I'm obleeged to you, and that's a fact. There's not many as would've tried to climb through that dormer window. And if you'll forgive me saying so, ma'am, you're a real 'eroine."

"She is that," Adam said.

Marianne spun around in time to watch Adam Jenson swing his powerful legs over the windowsill, then climb into the room. Seeing him standing there, whole and unharmed, she felt an almost overwhelming urge to run to him and throw her arms around his neck. Fortunately, she managed to subdue that urge before she made a fool of herself.

"If anyone deserves to be called a hero," she said, "that someone is Georgie. After all, *he* accomplished what I could not."

"But you tried, ma'am. And I won't never forget that it was you as 'ad the good sense to bring up the rope."

Having endured enough of this conversation, Marianne instructed Hannah to help Ben stretch out on the bed. "That wound needs to be seen to immediately. Can you clean it and stitch it closed?"

"I can, miss."

Though Ben apologized for making a nuisance of himself, he allowed Hannah to lead him to the bed, then he fell back against the pillows as though his strength had just about deserted him.

Later, while Hannah cleaned, stitched, and bandaged the gash in Ben's leg, Vince Sims stood just inside the bedchamber door, and though his face revealed nothing, he silently wrung his hat into a shapeless mass between his hands. After the ministrations to his son were completed, he touched his forelock politely to Hannah, shook Adam's hand, bowed to Marianne, then went outside, where he climbed aboard his cart and drove home to fetch his other son.

As soon as the elder Sims left the room, Marianne took Adam down to the kitchen, where he could wash up a bit, and once they were gone, Ben Sims looked about him at the master bedchamber. "It's a real nice room," he said.

"It is that," Hannah replied, "but no nicer than Miss McCord deserves." Warming to the subject, Hannah added, "She's been good to me and Georgie, so you be warned, Ben Sims. I won't hear nothing against her, not even from an injured man."

"Did I say aught against 'er? I think not."

"And you'd better not! Miss McCord is a real lady, and she don't deserve to be shunned by the villagers like she is. She can't help it if she's an orphan with no family to come live with her."

"No," Ben said, "don't reckon anybody'd be an orphan if they could 'elp it."

He looked around him once again, and his attention followed the sunlight that came through the bedchamber window. The light shone directly on the portrait above the fireplace, illuminating the lady in panniers and the three little children. "That little girl on the right must be Miss McCord's mother. Got them same gray-green eyes."

Hannah turned to look at the portrait, then she laughed. "Your injury has made you daft as a loon, Ben Sims, for that painting is at least sixty years old. Miss

McCord's mother wasn't even born when that was painted."

"Then it's 'er grandma," he said. "Daft I may be, but I got eyes in my 'ead, and that little girl is the spittin image of Miss McCord."

# Nine

While Hannah saw to it that Ben ate every bite of the sandwiches she had brought up for him, Marianne and Adam took their food outside, where they sat shoulder to shoulder on the sawhorse Vince Sims had neglected to put back on his cart. Someone had placed Marianne's Gypsy hat and Adam's coat and waistcoat nearby, but the respective owners paid little heed to their lost belongings, choosing instead to concentrate on Hannah's delicious sandwiches.

For a time they ate in silence. At least they *spoke* very little. Marianne's thoughts were going faster than the Dover mail coach, and they echoed loudly inside her head. Not that she blamed herself overmuch; after all, less than an hour earlier Adam had been trapped on the roof, and she had been so frightened for his safety that she had tried to climb out the attic window.

Foolish, of course, to think she could rescue Adam Jenson.

More foolish still, she was very much afraid she would do it all again.

"What are you thinking?" he asked, surprising her into turning to look at him.

She dared not tell him her true thoughts—that she was remembering how frightened she had been for him, and how, when he stepped inside the bedchamber, she had ached to put her arms around him and feel his strong, unharmed body next to hers. Unable to tell him the truth, she tried in vain to think of some acceptable prevarication. The task proved impossible, for Adam sat there looking so full of life and so handsome that Marianne feared her heart would burst right out of her chest.

She had thought him the epitome of masculinity in his form-fitting coats, but that was before she beheld him in his shirtsleeves. With only the thin linen covering his wide shoulders and broad back, it was all Marianne could do to stop herself from running her hand across the yoke of the shirt to feel the perfect symmetry of the manly form beneath.

She resisted the temptation, of course, but Adam did not make it easy, especially since he had chosen to roll up the full sleeves of the once snow-white shirt, revealing strong, thick wrists and sun-bronzed forearms whose muscles bunched and relaxed each time he lifted the sandwich to his mouth. Worse yet, he had loosened his cravat and released the button at the neck of the shirt, effectively giving Marianne *carte blanche* to stare at the strong column of his throat.

And stare she did. Finally, when she thought she would go mad with the desire to touch him, she was saved by the recollection that he had come to Bibb Grange to ask her something.

"Ah, yes," he said when she reminded him of his errand, "I almost forgot. Do you ride?"

"Ride?"

"Yes. My friend, Mr. Llewellyn, wishes to become better acquainted with Miss Faye Havor, and with that objective in mind, he has come up with a scheme for an alfresco nuncheon tomorrow. Naturally, he does not wish to appear too particular in his attentions, for Lady Havor is just that sort of matchmaking female who sees an invitation for a ride in the park as a precursor to her daughter's nuptials."

Marianne suspected the gentleman was correct, but she refrained from giving voice to her suspicions. Instead, she said, "And my being able to ride fits into Mr. Llewellyn's scheme in some way?"

"It does, for Franklin thought it would be prudent to include another female in the party."

*Not this female!*

"I have no objection to obliging your friend, but I am persuaded that Lady Havor would not agree to an outing that included me."

Adam gave her that raised-eyebrow look. "You are such an innocent lamb. For the chance to snare a son-in-law with Franklin Llewellyn's wealth and connections, I suspect Lady Havor would agree to let her daughter hobnob with Medusa."

"How very flattering. I shall be careful not to let the comparison go to my head."

A burst of laughter was Adam's only response. "You did not answer my question. Do you ride?"

"Yes. But nothing like Miss Havor. My great-aunt kept only her carriage horses, so during my years in Wales, I rode only occasionally, and then on hired hacks."

"I think I can provide you with something better than some hired bone-setter. Actually, there is a rather sweet little mare at the Hall stables who should suit you nicely. I will have a groom bring her around tomorrow morning."

"You are very kind, sir, but I cannot allow you—"

"Allow me to what? Send you a decent mount? How

could you go with us otherwise? Surely you were not thinking of riding that animal who has nearly cost you your life on more than one occasion?"

"Bess?" Marianne could not suppress a smile at the thought of tossing a saddle on the mare. "Poor Bess. I hope you do not mean to malign her again."

"Malign her? Madam, there are not words vile enough to slander that bag of bones."

Having effectively vilified the animal, Adam popped the last bite of sandwich into his mouth, then he bent to retrieve his coat and waistcoat. When he straightened, he stood and took Marianne's hands in his, pulling her to her feet. "My friend," he said, "you were splendid today."

The simple words caught her by surprise, and to conceal from him the breathlessness caused by his touch, Marianne stared at his hands, which still held hers. To her dismay, both of his palms were bisected by red, angry lines. "Adam! You are injured."

"Rope burns," he said. "Nothing to signify."

When she would have protested that they *did* signify, he silenced her by lifting her hands, one at a time, to his lips. "One of the grooms will bring the mare around first thing tomorrow. In the meantime, lock your doors against further intruders, and if you should have need of me, send Georgie on the run."

As it turned out, Mr. Llewellyn's alfresco nuncheon had to be postponed, for it rained on and off for the next three days, turning the lanes into quagmires unfit for pleasure riding. Of course, life inside Bibb Grange was anything but a pleasure during those three days of downpours. Though Vince Sims had promised to see to the grange roof on the first dry day, that did not relieve the inhabitants of the house from the necessity of running back and forth each time it rained, emptying and replacing dozens of drip pans.

Naturally, the place was at sixes and sevens. Even so, Hannah noticed one morning that someone had been inside the house. She had just gotten on her knees to begin her weekly scrubbing of the steps and the handsome carved panels with their mythical and woodland creatures, when she called to Marianne, "Look here, miss, if you would."

"What is it?"

"Call me daft, but there's a muddy boot print here on this step that don't look like nothing you nor I could've left."

With a sense of foreboding, Marianne approached the stairs. It was as Hannah said, the boot print was both too long and too broad to have been made by either of the women. She reached down to touch it, hoping as she did so that it would prove to be an old print left the day Ben Sims had been injured. Unfortunately, her finger came away slightly soiled, for the mud was still a bit soft, indicating that it had been left there within the past few hours.

Marianne looked at the grayish mud on her finger, and for an instant she experienced that same insidious fear that had gripped her four nights before, prompting her to run and hide like a frightened rabbit. Fear was the cruelest of thieves, for once again it robbed her of her confidence. It made her hands shake and her mouth go dry as wool.

But only for a matter of moments!

While she struggled to regain control of her emotions, Marianne reminded herself that she had faced real dan-

ger when she was willing to climb through an attic win-
low to help three men stranded on her roof. She had
proven to herself that she could be brave if the occasion
required it. She had been tried, and she had not been
found wanting.

Vowing never again to be a victim of her own fears,
she made her way up the steps, Hannah right behind
her, and followed the ever-dimmer muddy prints as they
continued up the stairs and around the corridor to the
right. The prints stopped outside the door of the small
room Marianne had occupied the first few days of her
residence, before the master bedchamber had been
cleaned and aired.

She opened the door slowly, and to her relief she
found the room empty. The only signs of recent occupancy was one faint heel print and a drawer that was
slightly ajar in the chiffonier.

"Did you open that drawer, Hannah?"

"No, miss. I clean the empty rooms on odd weeks,
and this one was due for a dusting and an airing some-
time this week. Besides, there b'aint no reason to open
any of the drawers. There's nothing in them, as you and
I both know."

"But a stranger would not know that."

The moment the words left her mouth, Marianne
wished them back, for they sent chills up her spine.
Someone had been in the house. Again! And this time
they had been abovestairs while she slept.

Seeing the perplexed look on Hannah's face, Marianne told her about what had happened four nights earlier. "And though Butterball could have broken the lamp
while pursuing her mouse, the cat is not clever enough
to open a ledger and leave it facedown on the table."

"No, miss. Butterball's smart, but she's not *that*

smart. Only a human would look through your ledger though I've no notion why anyone would want to. Nor can I guess why anyone would search the house. It's not as if we'd anything of real value."

"I wish I had an answer for you. I have racked my brain for a logical explanation for the original break-in but I have found none. Now the fellow has returned."

Hannah seemed not to hear, she was too lost in thought. "If anything valuable was ever in that drawer, miss, it got thrown out when we took all the drawers and chests outside and dumped the vermin-riddled contents in the rubbish pile to be burned. Hmm," she said as if mulling the facts over in her brain. "I wonder what it is he's after."

"I have no idea. Nor can I guess who might wish to search the house."

"Well," Hannah said, "he's had two chances to murder us in our beds and didn't bother, so I guess he's not dangerous. Whoever he may be, though, I wish he'd learn to wipe his boots before he comes in here tracking mud."

Marianne felt a strong desire to hug Hannah's ever-practical neck. She had not told the housekeeper about the previous break-in because she had been afraid Hannah might become fearful and want to leave the grange. She should have known better!

"With your permission, miss, I'll see the doors are bolted from now on. Do you think we should tell anyone about this?"

Marianne did not have an opportunity to tell Hannah that she had informed Lord Jenson of the break-in, for at just that moment Georgie came running in from the kitchen, his face pink with excitement, and announced

another unexpected caller. This time, however, the man was known to them.

"Mama," Georgie said, "Ben Sims is at the kitchen door, and he's got sommit for you and me. And if you please, miss, Ben says he would like to see you, too." His message delivered, the boy turned and sped back to the kitchen, leaving the women to follow at a more sedate pace.

When they entered the well-scrubbed, pleasant room, they found Ben Sims standing beside the welcoming fireplace, his bulky frame propped against the rough-hewn mantel. His longish brown hair was wet from the rain, and he had apparently left his boots outside, for his big feet were clad only in thick gray socks. He was smiling at Georgie, who sat at the deal table, gazing expectantly at a small package wrapped in butcher paper. There were two other packages on the table as well, one rather large, the other quite small.

The thatcher straightened when he saw the women and touched his forelock politely.

"Good morning, Ben."

"Morning, Miss McCord. And a bonnie morning to you, Miss 'Annah."

Hannah's cheeks turned a pretty pink. "What's all this, Ben Sims? Are you playing Father Christmas?"

The man looked down at his stocking feet and mumbled something about Hannah always having a sharp tongue. "Do you mean to let the boy open his gift?"

At his mother's nod, Georgie made short work of the wrapping paper. "Famous!" he shouted. "It's a cup and ball. I always wanted one."

The walnut cup, with its slender handle beneath, had been exquisitely carved and polished, as had the ball that fit into it. A hole had been bored through the ball, allow-

ing a long leather thong to pass through, and the object
of the toy was to swing the ball aloft and catch it in the
cup. No simple feat, as Georgie soon discovered.

"Excellent workmanship," Hannah said. "Did you
carve them, Ben?"

He nodded briefly, then informed her that the larger
package on the table was for her. "It's from my
grandma, so you don't need to worry about accepting
it. The smaller one is for you, miss. Grannie says to
tell you both she is obleeged to you for what you done
the day of the accident."

Marianne recalled the toothless old crone who had
slammed the door in her face the day she went in search
of the thatchers, but she saw no reason to hold the old
woman's rudeness against her grandson. Without allud-
ing to the incident at the cottage, Marianne sat at the
table and opened her gift.

Inside the paper lay a small square of snow-white
linen, its edges embroidered in softest pink and cream
and in one corner a beautifully executed "M." It was a
peace offering, and Marianne was more touched by the
gesture than she would have imagined. "Thank you
Ben. Please tell your grandmother that it is the loveliest
handkerchief I have ever owned."

"I'll tell 'er, ma'am."

Georgie abandoned the cup and ball long enough to
prod his mother to open her gift. "See what it is
Mama!"

Hannah did not copy her son's style of opening pre-
sents; instead, she took her time, choosing to handle the
paper with care so that it might be saved for future use.
When she finally folded back the overlapping edges
she discovered a fringed shawl woven in shades of rust
and green.

"When Grannie was deciding on the thread for 'er loom, I told 'er you 'ad a dress in them colors back when you were no bigger than Georgie there."

Hannah blushed profusely. "You remembered that? After all this time?"

He nodded. "I always thought it looked real nice with your hair."

"You did?"

"Always."

Hannah said nothing more, merely shook out the soft wool garment, draped it reverently about her shoulders, then turned first one way then the other so everyone could see the effect.

Like Marianne and Georgie, Ben watched Hannah turn to and fro, but his attention was not on the shawl. The thatcher's gaze never left Hannah's face. "You look fine as five pence," he said quietly.

Perceiving that she was definitely de trop, Marianne thanked the visitor once again for her handkerchief, then she excused herself and exited the kitchen. Half an hour later, she happened to be looking out her bedchamber window and saw Ben Sims walking down the carriage-way toward the lane. His visit with Hannah must have gone well, for he whistled happily, apparently unaware of the rain that soon soaked through his jacket and hat, or the mud that *squished* beneath his boots.

While the thatcher walked toward the village, growing wetter by the minute, Adam Jenson sat in the toasty comfort of his book room, reading a letter only just come from London. The missive was from Mr. Phineas Hildebrandt, his man of business, and though the solicitor did not answer all the questions Adam had posed in his own letter, he had quite a bit to say regarding Mr. Titus Brougham.

*Sir,*

*As you asked, I inquired among a few people who know these kind of things, and I discovered one or two interesting facts about Mr. Titus Brougham. He came into his inheritance some five years ago, but the Brougham estate was modest and the profits were soon spent in gentlemanly but financially ruinous pursuits.*

*About two years ago, he sold an emerald reportedly brought back from India by his maternal grandfather, and he has been living off the proceeds of that sale ever since.*

*As I understand it, those monies are now depleted. Once again, the gentleman has amassed some rather serious debts, and the holder of the majority of his vowels is a rather nasty fellow who employs known thugs to collect what is owed him.*

*As for Mr. Brougham's reason for being in Chelmford, that I cannot say with any degree of certainty. I will hazard a guess, however, that his rather abrupt desertion of London for Derbyshire had something to do with his debts, which are reported to exceed three thousand pounds.*

*Is there, perhaps, a young lady in the area who is in possession of a handsome dowry?*

*In regard to your questions about an army lieutenant by the name of Marcus Wilson, I have discovered nothing yet, but I will continue to hound the Home Secretary until I have the information you require.*

*Until then, I am yr. obd. svt,*
*Phineas Hildebrandt, Esq.*

Adam folded the letter and placed it on top of the desk. "So," he said, his words low and meant for himself alone, "it is as I suspected, Brougham is in debt. But what, I wonder, can he possibly want with Marianne McCord? By her own admission, the lady is in possession of nothing of value."

"What is this?" Mr. Llewellyn asked, lowering the four-day-old newspaper he had been perusing by the hearth. "Surely you are aware, old boy, of what becomes of fellows who talk to themselves? Their relatives send them to Bedlam. Not that I suspect Lady Jenson of wishing to lock you up, but if you will carry on conversations with yourself, I shall feel it my duty to inform your lady mother of the practice."

"Do shut up, Franklin. I am trying to think."

"Don't do it," his friend cautioned. "Thinking always leads a man into trouble."

Adam motioned negligently toward the letter on his desk. "My man of business seems to believe that Titus Brougham's sudden arrival in Chelmford might have to do with his possible pursuit of a young lady with a sizable dowry."

"Damn his eyes!" Mr. Llewellyn said, tossing the newspaper aside and getting to his feet in some agitation. "The varlet has come to try his luck with Miss Havor!"

Though Adam did not share Mr. Llewellyn's belief that Brougham had come to Derbyshire to fix his interest with Faye Havor, he was intrigued by the degree of agitation the idea caused his friend. "Do I detect a note of jealousy there, Franklin?"

"Not at all, old boy. It is merely that I admire Miss Havor far too much to wish to see her fall under the influence of a man like Brougham—a man who would

not know how to appreciate the lady's unique qualities. In fact," he added, crossing the room toward the door, "I believe I will ride over to Haybury House right away, just to drop a hint in Sir Percival's ear about Mr. Titus Brougham."

"Franklin," Adam said, stopping his friend before he left the room, "are you forgetting the state of the weather?"

It was obvious that the gentleman's wish to visit the Havors had pushed from his mind all recollection of the rain, for when he glanced out of the windows that offered a view of the side garden, his blue eyes widened with surprise at the precipitation.

One look at the momentary indecision on Franklin's face, and Adam was hard pressed not to howl with laughter. "Dampened your ardor, did it?"

"A mere drizzle," Mr. Llewellyn said, his tone determined once again. "A bit too damp to ride, of course, but a walk would do me no harm."

"It is four miles, my friend."

"Nothing to it, old boy. After being cooped up here for three days, I am persuaded I will enjoy the exercise."

"You think that, do you? I begin to suspect it is *you* who will end his life a Bedlamite."

Mr. Llewellyn paid him not the least attention. "I believe I saw a stash of rain gear in that little cloakroom where the fishing rods are stored. Think I'll have a look to see if any of it will fit me."

Adam was still smiling at his friend's all-too-transparent excuse to call upon Miss Havor, when it occurred to him that he, too, was feeling the need of a bit of exercise. Not bothering to examine his own motives, he waited ten minutes to give Franklin time to be on his

way, then walked rather purposefully from the book room.

"I think I shall take a stroll," he said to the startled footman who directed him to the cloakroom containing the rain gear, "just to see how they are getting along at Bibb Grange."

# Ten

The sound of the knocker surprised Marianne, but not nearly as much as her discovery of Viscount Jenson standing outside her front door, rain glistening from an oilcloth slicker well past its prime and mud halfway up a pair of disreputable rain boots. Surprise gave way to amusement, which was instantly displaced by sheer pleasure at seeing her neighbor, no matter what his outer wear.

She had vowed more than once to keep Adam Jenson at arm's distance, but those vows were apparently forgotten, for she opened the door wide and bid him come in.

"Are you quite sure?" Adam asked, glancing down at the mud-caked boots. "I should hate to have Hannah ring a peal over me for tracking up the floors."

"I would not worry if I were you, sir, for Hannah said nothing this morning when Ben Sims stopped in."

"Ben came, did he? In the rain?" He laughed. "There must be an epidemic."

Marianne had no idea to what Adam referred, but she did not care. It was enough that he was there, and that with his coming the ennui that had gripped her for the past several days was miraculously gone. "Of course," she added, "Hannah's acceptance of the thatcher's visit

owed much to the fact that he removed his shoes before he walked across the floor. Oh, and he also came bearing gifts."

Adam stopped in his removal of the rain-soaked slicker. "Gifts! Madam, if that is a hint, allow me to remind you that the first time I came to Bibb Grange, I brought you *four* cats. According to my reckoning, that means I am still one gift to the good."

"True, sir, but the felines were all in *one* basket. Surely that signifies—"

"What it signifies," he said, "is that I brought four *gifts,* all of them in one *basket.*"

He laid the slicker on the floor and removed first one boot, then the other. "Now, may we table this discussion of gifts until some more appropriate time, like Boxing Day, so that I may join you in whatever room you were occupying before I arrived? Preferably one with a carpet on the floor."

After staring at his stocking feet—the second pair she had seen that day—she bid him come into the parlor. They went immediately to the inglenook with its carved seats and cheerful blue-and-white upholstery. Marianne had lit a small fire just before Adam arrived, one that would not smoke the room past endurance if the wind should change direction, and the enclosed area was now snug and inviting.

They sat opposite each another, and while Marianne reclaimed the pillow slip she had been mending and plied her needle, Adam stretched his long legs toward the fire, his ankles crossed and his feet resting on a small petit-point stool. It was exactly the sort of scene Marianne had imagined thousands of times since she was old enough to dream, with her sewing and the man she loved lounging beside the—

*The man she loved!*

Where had that thought come from? It had come unbidden, of course, and yet so naturally that it took Marianne's breath away. She loved Adam Jenson. It was true; no point in denying it. She loved him, and she suspected she had loved him for quite some time.

*Aunt Gertrude, you sanctimonious old hen, you were right. Like my mother, I fell in love with the one man guaranteed to break my heart.*

"Tuppence for your thoughts," Adam said.

His voice sounded mesmerizingly relaxed, and to guard against falling under its spell, Marianne answered with the first thing that popped into her head. "I was thinking of feet. Men's feet, that is. They seem to be playing a rather interesting part in my life today."

"Feet? Mine and Ben's, you mean?"

"Actually, there is a third pair, though I am unable to supply the name of the owner."

Adam sat up straight, all semblance of relaxation gone. "Tell me," he said.

She told him about the muddy footprints Hannah had discovered on the steps and about finding the drawer ajar in the small bedchamber. "It was the same man who broke in before. I am convinced of it."

"And he was searching for something abovestairs? Have you any idea what?"

"None whatsoever. The first week I was here, Hannah and I cleaned the house from top to bottom, and we found nothing worth stealing."

"Did he force his way in? Perhaps pry open a window?"

"We found scratches on the jamb of the kitchen door, but the wood is so old, the marring may have occurred

years ago. Otherwise, there were no signs of forced entry."

Adam was quiet for a moment, as if contemplating something, then he asked her to look carefully at his foot. "Try to recall the size of the print left by the boot. Would my foot fit into such a shoe?"

Despite the seriousness of their discussion, Marianne felt a strong desire to giggle. "Sir, you have a very impressive foot."

"Thank you," he said as if accepting a compliment. "And the print on the stair?"

"Oh, not nearly so impressive, I promise you."

He ignored her sarcasm. "That corroborates something I already suspected."

"And that is?"

"Let us review what we have here. Firstly, from his boot size, we know the man has smallish feet, which probably means he is short, or at least not as tall as I am. Secondly, he may have prior knowledge of the house, at least enough to know how to get in without using force. And thirdly, since he has not so far made off with anything, it would appear he is after something in particular."

*"He,"* Marianne said. "You speak the pronoun as though you knew the actual name. Whom do you suspect?"

"Who else? Titus Brougham."

Somehow, Marianne was not surprised. "Though I am perfectly willing to accept that Mr. Brougham is guilty of all manner of nefarious acts, I should like to hear why *you* suspect him of breaking into my house? And what motive could he have for searching it?"

"I cannot be sure, of course, but I believe he hopes

to find a jewel here at Bibb Grange. One worth several thousand pounds."

"Here? A jewel worth several thousand pounds? What on earth put such a fanciful notion into your head? Or into his, for that matter?"

"I have it on good authority that Brougham sold a very valuable emerald several years ago—something brought from India by his maternal grandfather, a nabob, no doubt. Since the emerald came to Brougham from his mother's side of the family—the Bibb family—perhaps the nabob brought back more than one gem from India. And if he did, perhaps the other stone was in Mr. Theodore Bibb's possession."

"If such a stone existed, would Mr. Bibb not have left it to his nephew, his only living relative?"

Adam gave her a long look, that eyebrow raised as if to mock her naivety. "He did not leave *Bibb Grange* to his nephew."

Not at all happy with where this conversation was going, Marianne lifted the gold chain from beneath the fichu at her neck and showed Adam the little filigree acorn with the green stone locked inside, holding it between her fingers so he could see it. "This is the only jewel I possess. It was my mother's, and even if it should prove to be an emerald, which I doubt, it is not large enough to tempt someone to come down from London to steal it."

Without so much as a by-your-leave, Adam left his place on the opposite side of the inglenook and joined Marianne on the other carved bench, sitting very close to her. She still held the little gold acorn between her fingers, and he put his hand beneath hers, letting the trinket rest in his palm.

Even with him sitting so close to her, Marianne might

have retained her composure had the back of Adam's large, very masculine hand not rested against her throat. At the feel of his warm flesh touching hers, all coherent thought vanished from her mind. Unfortunately, her ladylike inhibitions disappeared as well—those inhibitions that were supposed to keep females from experiencing wanton feelings—and Marianne found herself leaning toward Adam, her face lifted to his.

Adam had been concentrating on the green stone inside the golden acorn, attempting to turn it so the light from the fire would fall on it, when he felt Marianne lean toward him ever so slightly. At first he thought she had shifted to allow him a better look at the gold fob, but the next instant an alarm bell clanged in his head, rung by that animal instinct that alerts males to possibly willing females.

He looked at her, at her lovely face and her full, slightly parted lips, and a pulse began to beat at the base of his ears, the noise so loud, it all but deafened him. She wanted to be kissed, and God help him, Adam wanted to kiss her. He wanted it so badly, it hurt.

Unfortunately, he knew, even if she did not, that one kiss would never be enough. Not after all those amorous dreams he had been having lately—dreams of passionate kisses beside a gently flowing brook; of heated embraces beneath a shaded tree; of ardent lovemaking on satin sheets—dreams that always included the same female, Miss Marianne McCord.

If Adam took her in his arms now, here in this cozy inglenook, he knew he would be unable to release her until after he had made her his, and that would spell disaster. Disaster for him, and ruin for the beautiful innocent who was his neighbor and his friend. Her youth had been tainted by the stigma of illegitimacy, and

Adam would not sully what remained of her reputation by adding her name to his list of paramours.

"Miss?" said a child's high-pitched voice. "Mama wants to know if you would like a cuppa tea and a sandwich to— Oh. Your lordship. We didn't know you were here, sir."

Adam breathed a sigh of relief. *Saved by a child!*

Marianne sighed too, but if Adam was any judge, her emotions were far different from his. "That would be nice," she said, her voice edged with frustration. "Thank you, Georgie."

The boy did not leave immediately, but asked, "Shall I bring enough for his lordship?"

"Yes, *thank you,* Georgie. That will be all."

When the lad left the room, Marianne spoke again, and this time a hint of anger crept into her voice. "This is all your fault, Adam Jenson. Were it not for you, that boy would be in school, not here, interrupting what might have been a wonderful—"

"What!" Understandably, Adam was taken aback by her quite baseless accusation. Thinking it best to ignore the final part of her statement—the part he truly wished to explore—he concentrated instead on the first. "Georgie's schooling, or lack thereof, has nothing to do with me."

"Of course it does. It was you who closed the village school."

"I never!"

"Bob Quimby said you did, and he should know."

"*I* tell you, I did not. I did not even know there *was* a school in the village. And who the devil is Bob Quimby?"

"Who the—" Marianne paused as if unable to believe

his question. "Bob Quimby manages the mill. Surely you know your own employees."

"What a nonsensical notion. I do not even know the names of all the servants at Jenson Park in Kent and I have lived there all my life. My mother lives there still. So why the deuce should I know a bunch of mill workers here in Derbyshire?"

From the way her eyes grew wide with disbelief, an onlooker would be forgiven for thinking Adam had said something quite outrageous. He had not, of course, but Marianne stared at him as though Venus, or some other equally startling manifestation, had just sprung from his head.

"Perhaps I misunderstood you," she said. "Did you mean to say that you know only the master weavers at the mill?"

"I meant nothing of the sort."

"But . . . but they work for you. Their labor provides at least a portion of your wealth, and their livelihood— the very food in their children's mouths—depends upon employment in your mill."

Adam knew a moment of discomfort. For some reason, he didn't like losing Marianne's admiration, and he could tell from the way she had suddenly averted her eyes, choosing not to look at him, that he had disappointed her. "The water-powered mill and the model village were my grandfather's project. My own father had little interest in either the village or the mill. So little, in fact, that he seldom visited Chelmford. As far as I can recall, he brought me here only once, and that was to see my grandfather laid to rest."

"I see," she said, the words very quiet.

"No," he said, "I do not think you understood at all."

Nor was Adam at all certain he could explain it to

her satisfaction. Had it not been for his grandfather's wealth and title, the Fifth Viscount Jenson would have been shunned by society for owning a mill. Nobles and gentry alike would have said he "smelled of the shop." Not that his grandfather cared what anyone said or thought of him! That bullheaded old martinet would have relegated the whole of society to Hades without batting an eye.

Not so the sixth viscount.

Adam's father cared very much what was said of him, as did his wife, and they took great pains to protect their status among the *ton*. As for Adam, until ten seconds earlier he had not given much thought to either his grandfather's or his father's choices. Adam was a wealthy viscount, and as such he had taken his place in society. Unlike his father, however, the social whirl was not the be-all and end-all of Adam's existence. If the truth be told, in the past few years the endless round of parties and the same predictable conversations had become more and more tedious.

That was all beside the point, of course, for Adam was not obliged to explain himself or his actions to anyone, not even to Marianne McCord.

He had not spoken for several minutes, nor had Marianne, and when she rose from the settle and walked over to stare out the front-facing window, leaving him and the warmth of the inglenook, Adam stood as well and followed her. He stopped just behind her, only inches between them, and placed his hands on her soft, feminine shoulders. When she did not shrug his hands away, he moved even closer and rested his chin on the top of her head.

"Must we let this ruin our day?" he asked softly. "Is it so important?"

"That is a question you should ask yourself," she said, her voice cooler than he had ever heard it. "You must be aware of the fact that everything you do or say influences these people's lives. *I* consider that an awesome responsibility, but only *you* know whether or not it is important to you."

Before Adam could reply to her observation, he heard footfalls in the corridor just outside the parlor, so he released Marianne's shoulders and stepped back.

"Your tea and sandwiches, miss," Hannah said from the doorway. "Shall I put the tray on the table or take it over to the inglenook so you can sit by the fire?"

"Set it on the table, Hannah, then be so good as to pour his lordship a cup of tea. I have the headache, and I really must excuse myself from remaining belowstairs another moment."

She turned to Adam then and curtsied in the manner of a polite stranger. "You will excuse me, my lord. Thank you so much for stopping by."

With that, she walked to the door, exited the room, and disappeared up the staircase, leaving Adam staring after her, disbelief robbing him of speech. *How dare she judge him!*

"Sir," Hannah said hesitantly, "shall I pour the—"

"Go!" he said, finally finding his voice. The startled housekeeper must have sensed the growing fury inside him, fury only just held in check, for she made short work of escaping his presence. Adam could hear her footfalls as she ran down the corridor toward the back of the house.

Resisting the temptation to take the stairs two at a time, then throw open Marianne's bedchamber door and throttle her, Adam strode instead to the vestibule. Once he had reclaimed his disreputable rain gear, he marched

from the house, slamming the heavy oak door behind him for good measure.

Several hours later, Adam sat in a comfortable wing chair beside the hearth in his bedchamber, his slippered feet stretched toward the fire that crackled enticingly. It was a proper blaze, warm and inviting, not like that paltry excuse for a fire at Bibb Grange.

But then, what could one expect in the home of a female totally lacking in sense, completely devoid of all social graces, and utterly deficient in knowledge of the world and how it operated? "How dare she take me to task!"

And how dare she walk out on him as though he were of no more importance than a peddler on the street. More furious than he could remember being in his entire life, he poured himself a glass of the brandy his valet had brought on a tray earlier while he had soaked in the hip bath filled with steaming water.

"The brandy will keep away the chill, my lord," the servant had said.

Not that Adam was chilled. Far from it! Not surprisingly, his anger kept him warm, just as it had during the wet, muddy half-mile trek back to the Hall. At the reminder of his ignominious departure from Bibb Grange, Adam swore and threw the glass, brandy and all, against the Italian marble fireplace. The crystal shattered into hundreds of pieces—pieces that flew in every direction—while the amber liquid slowly ran down the pale green marble to puddle on the hearth.

"How dare she!"

As if *she,* a little nobody, had every right to look disdainfully at *him.* He was a viscount after all. If any-

one had a right to be disillusioned, it was Adam, for Marianne McCord was obviously not the warm, generous person he had thought her to be.

By the time every last drop of the spilled brandy had run down the marble face of the fireplace, Adam was congratulating himself on his wisdom in resisting Marianne's laughably awkward attempt to seduce him into kissing her. So gauche. So unladylike.

Were he not such a gentleman, the conclusion of their encounter in the inglenook would have been far different. He thanked heaven that he had seen the true Marianne before their relationship had gone any further.

Gratitude for his fortunate escape soon gave way to a recollection of the woman's full, parted lips; of the feel of her soft shoulders beneath his hands; and of the sweet, clean, womanly smell of her. At that all-too-vivid recollection, Adam's anger became all mixed up with the desire that lurked just beneath the surface—desire too easily rekindled by the least thought of Marianne McCord.

"Damn her!"

"Who?" Mr. Llewellyn asked.

Adam turned quickly to glower at his houseguest. "Do you never knock?"

"I knocked, old boy, but you did not hear. You were talking to yourself again, though I warned you earlier where that would lead."

After calling his friend by a vile epithet, Adam invited him to take the seat on the other side of the hearth. "There is brandy if you want it."

Mr. Llewellyn took the proffered seat, but he refused the offer of a drink. After eyeing the stained marble and the fragments of crystal peppered about the carpet, he said, "Bad vintage, was it?"

Adam ignored the question. From the lateness of Franklin's return to Jenson Hall, not to mention the smile that appeared to have become a permanent part of the man's face, Adam assumed his friend was already drunk on something, though he did not think it was wine. Apparently, Franklin's reception at Havor House, after walking through the rain and mud, had proved more felicitous than Adam's visit to Bibb Grange.

"Sir Percival and Lady Havor are in good health, I presume?"

"They are quite well. Though bored with this inclement weather."

"And Miss Havor? She, too, is in good health?"

"Oh, yes."

"And happy to see you, I've no doubt."

"I believe she was. We spent the entire afternoon together, talking and playing silly children's games by the fire. It was great fun."

"And what of the young lady's mama? Did she play games as well, or did she spend the afternoon composing an announcement for the *Times?*"

Franklin picked up a leather-bound book from the small mahogany table beside his chair and threw the volume at Adam's head.

Adam deflected the missile with his arm and laughed for the first time since early afternoon. "A simple no would have sufficed."

His friend settled back in his chair, a sigh upon his lips. "Adam, she is the most delightful young lady."

"Lady Havor?"

"Do be serious, old boy. You must know I mean Faye. Miss Havor, I should say."

"Ah, yes, the fair Miss Havor. The young lady's hair is blond, I believe you said."

"Yes, and she is angelically fair. At least *I* think so. She might not suit everyone's taste, mind you, for she's a bit on the tall side, but she's a darling for all that."

"And an excellent rider."

"Quite. By the way, we rescheduled the alfresco nuncheon for two days following the last day of rain. I assumed you and Miss McCord would have no objection."

Apparently not noticing that he received no corroboration of his assumption, Franklin began to reel off a catalogue of Miss Faye Havor's talents and attributes. The list was long, and he spoke at length, beginning each sentence with "Miss Havor" this, or "Miss Havor" that.

Adam heard little of what was actually said, for at the mention of Marianne's name, he had begun to remember, one by one, all the reasons why he liked her. Her wit. Her honesty. Her genuineness. Her indomitable spirit. Her bravery. Her smile.

His catalogue of Marianne's virtues was not as long as Franklin's list of Miss Havor's talents, but it was enough to affect Adam's anger, causing it to subside ever so slowly. When it disappeared entirely, so did his resentment, and he was free to think seriously about Marianne's chastisement of him and the disappointment he had seen in her eyes. When Franklin finally fell silent and stared into the fire, as if captivated by the bright orange-and-blue flames, Adam said, "Will you tell me something?"

"Anything, old boy."

"Your father has a number of tenants on his estate. Does he know them all by name?"

"What a foolish question."

Adam breathed a sigh of relief, feeling somewhat vindicated. "I thought it might be foolish, but—"

"Naturally he knows their names, as do I, and the names of their children as well. Why, I'm even on a first-name basis with old Bart Whaley's pointers, especially Miss Blue. Prettiest bitch you ever saw. I remember one time when my father and I were in pursuit of a covey of quail, Miss Blue caught the scent—"

"Hell's bells, Franklin, I have no wish to hear about some blasted hound! I was curious to know about your father's relationship with his tenants."

Franklin gave him a surprised look. "What is there to know? They depend on us and we depend on them."

"As simple as that?"

"And as complex. Some of the families, like the Whaleys, have been on the land for six or eight generations. I have known them all my life, just as they have known me. And believe me, sometimes they know too damn much about a fellow!"

"How so?"

"I recall one night in particular, when I was about twelve years old, Bart Whaley's two oldest boys and I decided it would be a great lark if we went for a swim in the village pond. As it turned out, the joke was on us, for while we were in the water, naked as the day we were born, one of the tavern maids came by and stole our clothes. You can imagine the uproar it caused when the three of us were obliged to return to our respective homes dressed in nothing save a few strategically placed oak leaves."

Adam laughed. "What of your clothes? Did you ever get them back?"

"Oh, yes. The next day they were nailed to the door of the tavern for all to see. For my part, I wanted to

forget the clothes. Not so my father. Always a fair man, he insisted that since the Whaley brothers had to retrieve their clothes, so must I. Furthermore, he said I was to share whatever punishment was meted out to the others."

"Which was?"

"To ensure that we not soon forget our disgraceful behavior, Bart Whaley insisted his lads buy a pint for the first two men who entered the tavern. Naturally, I had to buy a pint for the third man. As you can imagine, by nightfall every family in the county was laughing at the story.

"They still do," he said, a smile on his face. "Just let me go into the tavern for a pint or two, and before long, someone will tell the story of our midnight bath in the public pond."

"If that is the case, why not simply avoid the place? Why put yourself through the humiliation?"

His friend looked at him as if he had asked an idiotic question. "Who said anything about humiliation? Each time the story is retold, I laugh as hard as anyone else in the tavern. Why would I not? The episode in the pond, the village itself, and those people are all a part of my life. As they will one day be a part of my son's life. And when that day comes, I hope I am as good a landlord as my father, one who knows his tenants, appreciates their contribution to his lifestyle, and in return looks out for their welfare."

Franklin continued, albeit hesitantly. "Your grandfather shared my father's philosophy."

Surprised, Adam said, "What do you know of the fifth viscount?"

"Only what I have heard my father say. He admired

your grandfather and followed with interest the fate of the water-powered mill and the model village."

"And what of my *father?* Did your father admire him as well?"

Franklin ran a finger inside the collar of his shirt, whose points appeared to have grown higher and far too snug. "I never heard him mention your father."

"A diplomatic answer, my friend. And what of me? I suppose he thinks me a social fribble like my father."

Franklin shook his head. "There is much of your grandfather in you, Adam. You just have not realized it yet."

"You quite mistake the matter."

"Then, why did you climb up on Miss McCord's roof to help the two stranded thrashers?"

"Oh, that. I beg of you, do not give me any great degree of credit for that. My reasons were simple. I had sent the men up there, so they were, in essence, my responsibility."

"My point exactly, old boy. It all boils down to a person's perception of responsibility."

# Eleven

Marianne had not slept at all well the previous two nights, the cause of her insomnia a combination of disillusionment and disappointment. She was still disillusioned by Adam Jenson's lack of interest in the welfare of the villagers, but she was also experiencing a growing disappointment in her own behavior toward him. The more she relived the afternoon in the blue and white parlor, when Adam had come to see her, the more she began to doubt the justness of her outrage.

Who was she to criticize him? She knew nothing of the lives of people with great wealth, or of the responsibility such people felt toward those who worked for them, and lately an idea had been niggling at her brain, a suspicion that she might have been unfair to Adam.

She had judged him, applying the same mindless standards that others had used to judge her, and for something he could not help any more than she could— an accident of birth. The growing regret she felt as a result of her self-righteous behavior was robbing Marianne of much-needed sleep.

Sunday night she lay in bed for the better part of two hours, tossing and turning and accomplishing nothing except making a shambles of the sheets. During that time, she toyed with the idea of writing Adam a note

begging his pardon, going so far as to compose at least a dozen versions of the apology in her head. Unsure about the note, she tabled the idea for the moment, choosing instead to go belowstairs to the kitchen for a cup of warm milk.

Hoping the milk might make her drowsy, she threw back the covers, slipped her feet into her felt house slippers, then lit the candle beside her bed. Unfortunately, when she opened her bedchamber door, a slight puff of wind blew out the candle flame.

"Drat!" she muttered.

Deciding she knew her way well enough in the dark to dispense with the light, she walked slowly toward the staircase, sliding her hand along the wall to guide her. Because her soft felt slippers gave her a firm feel for the stairs, she made it all the way to the bottom without mishap. She had only just turned the corner to follow the short corridor to the kitchen, when she bumped into something solid and unyielding.

"Umph!" the object said.

Convinced that she had collided with a person, and certain that person was male, Marianne stepped back, her legs trembling as though her bones had turned to aspic. All would have been well if the man had turned and run; unfortunately, he did not. He grabbed for Marianne, and at the feel of his grasping fingers closing around her wrist, she drew a deep breath and screamed loud enough to wake the inhabitants in the next county.

" 'Sblood!" the man said, the profanity muffled. "Quiet!"

Marianne drew breath to scream again, and within an instant she felt the man's fist slam into the side of her head. For the briefest of seconds, she stood quite still, unable to believe that she had been struck. Then, as a

million shards of pain exploded inside her brain, she felt her knees give way and the floor rise up to meet her. Thankfully, before she actually hit the floor, she lost consciousness and drifted into blessed oblivion.

"Miss," Hannah said. "Oh, miss, please wake up."

The housekeeper held Marianne's hand, giving it a series of quick pats every few seconds, as if that might waken her. For some reason Marianne did not immediately comprehend, she and Hannah were both on the floor, with the three kittens sniffing at them as though curious to know what had happened.

Georgie stood above them, a candlestick in his hand, and if his whispered questions were anything to go by, he was every bit as curious as the kittens. Because the candlelight hurt Marianne's eyes, she let her lids fall shut once again.

"Is she dead, Mama?"

"Hush, son."

"She looks dead."

"Well, she b'aint, so I'll thank you to keep that light still and your mouth closed."

"I am alive," Marianne said, "but the light hurts my eyes."

"Shield the candle, Georgie." Once the boy had done her bidding, Hannah put her arm beneath Marianne's shoulders and helped her to sit up. "We heard you scream, miss. Did you fall?"

Marianne did not answer right away, for when she sat up, her head swam and she was overcome by a wave of nausea. After she took several deep gulps of air, however, the nausea subsided and she was able to tell Hannah about bumping into the man. "Then he hit me,"

she said, "and I knew nothing more until you told me to wake up."

Hannah bid Georgie bring the candle close so she could examine Marianne's head, then with cautious fingers she lifted aside the thick tresses. "There's a bump rising, miss, but the skin isn't broken. Likely you'll have the headache for a few hours, and you'll do well to brush your hair real gentle like tomorrow. Otherwise, you've come to no real harm."

*No real harm!* For once Marianne did not appreciate Hannah's practical approach. Considering the fright she had had and the injury sustained, Marianne felt that a bit of sympathy was in order, but apparently her housekeeper had other matters on her mind.

"I'll help you up to your bed, miss, and if you like, me and Georgie can sleep in the little room across the corridor. Though I've no doubt the man is long gone by now. The way you screamed, it probably scared him out of his wits. It did me, and that's a fact."

"Me too," Georgie offered. "I never knew a grown lady could scream so loud. Like as not, miss, they heard you all the way up at the Hall."

Running out of patience with the two Job's comforters, Marianne declined Hannah's offer of support and asked Georgie merely to light her up to her bedchamber. Once there, she lit an entire brace of candles, wished the boy a good night, then closed the door behind him and turned the key, not caring one whit that he heard her lock herself in.

Georgie had mentioned the Hall, and since Marianne did not share the boy's opinion that their closest neighbor had probably heard her scream, she decided to write

that note she had been vacillating about. Adam had told her to send word if there were any more break-ins, and though that was before they argued, she convinced herself that she was merely doing as he asked.

After seating herself resolutely at the Queen Anne desk, she pulled out the slide on the left side of the desk, set the brace of candles on it, then took a sheet of vellum from the stack and opened the crockery ink pot on the pewter tray. Once she dipped the stylus in the black liquid, however, her resolve seemed to vanish. *My Lord,* she began, *I apologize for . . .*

Muttering beneath her breath, Marianne wadded the vellum into a tight ball and threw it across the room. It landed beneath the portrait of the lady and her three children.

Claiming a new sheet of vellum, Marianne began anew. *Sir, I may have been a bit hasty when last we met . . .* Muttering again, she wadded the second sheet into a ball and threw it after the first. Five more starts resulted in five more vellum balls, each one flung with more frustration than the one before it.

It was no use, she could not write to Adam. How could she berate a man one day, then three days later ask for his help? She could not.

There must be some other way to rid herself of the intruder—some way short of nailing a sign to the front door informing any who cared to know that there were no valuable jewels at Bibb Grange. Forty minutes later, when that other way still had not presented itself, Marianne closed the ink pot and put the stylus away.

With the brace of candles in hand, she crossed the room and began to retrieve the wads of vellum, calling herself a fool for having thrown them in the first place. It was when she picked up the final ball of paper, which

had landed just below the portrait, that she saw something about the painting she had never noticed before.

Holding the candles a mere inch from the canvas, she inspected the lady with the panniers and the powdered wig. Years of grime, aided by smoke from the fireplace, had blackened the portrait, all but obscuring portions of it, and it was in bad need of cleaning. With the light held close, however, Marianne could make out a greenish clip of some sort adorning the rather elaborate wig. No, two clips. One was near the lady's right temple, the other to her left, just above a sausage curl that trailed over her bare shoulder.

Inspecting first one clip, then the other, Marianne stared at them until the strain of staring made her close her eyes and rub her fingertips across her lids. When she was convinced of what she saw, she returned to the desk and claimed the last piece of vellum from the stack that had once reposed on the corner of the smooth walnut surface.

*Adam,*
  *Please come to Bibb Grange as soon as possible.*
*I have found the second emerald.*

                                        *Marianne*


The next day was the sort of bright, sunny day that Englishmen cherish, especially after a full week of rain, so Marianne did not feel at all apologetic about sending Georgie over to Jenson Hall to deliver her note. Waiting for a reply, however, took its toll upon her nerves, and she was unable to swallow even a bite of the basted egg and popover Hannah had prepared for her.

Finally abandoning all pretense at breaking her fast,

Marianne pushed aside her plate and returned to the blue-and-white parlor, where she could stand at the window and watch for Adam. Impatient to know if he would come to her, or if he would throw her note into the fire and ignore her plea, she made a fine mess of the cording at the drapery, knotting and unknotting it until it began to fray at the ends.

At last she heard a noise on the carriageway. Unfortunately, it was the squeak of cart wheels, and though she was pleased to know that the thatchers had kept their promise and had returned to finish mending her roof, she was disappointed not to see Adam. Within less than a minute, the thatcher's two-wheeled cart came into view, filled once again with fresh straw. This time Vince Sims handled the ribbons, with Ben sitting on the hard plank seat beside him, and his other son—a young man of perhaps twenty—walking beside the cart.

Ben saw Marianne at the window, and when she nodded, he touched his finger to the bill of his cap. Vince Sims did not stop the cart in the front, as before, but drove it around to the rear of the house, where he immediately began to yell orders to his two sons.

"Get them tools unlashed, Gideon, there's a good lad, then put the ladder together and get started taking the tools atop the roof. And don't forget ter take up a length of rope with you first off. Only a fool makes the same mistake twice."

While the thatchers unloaded their cart and prepared to mend the roof at Bibb Grange, Adam Jenson descended the grand staircase at the Hall, his destination the morning room, where an elegant buffet was laid out each day.

"Good morning, my lord," Sykes said.

Before Adam could return the butler's greeting, he

was surprised into silence by a loud commotion coming from the nether regions of the Hall.

"Help!" yelled a voice that sounded suspiciously like Georgie Scott's. "Your lordship!"

"What on earth?"

Ignoring the butler's hurried offer to see what was amiss, Adam turned and strode purposefully down the long, carpeted corridor that led to the kitchen. At least he thought it was the kitchen; having never been there before, he was not altogether certain. The point was moot, however, for before he had covered half the distance, Georgie burst forward, rushing toward him, one of the footmen in pursuit.

"Sir," Georgie gasped, "I've a message for you, and that man is trying to take it from me."

Adam waved the footman away. "A message, you say?"

"Yes, sir. Miss told me I was to deliver it into your hand and no other."

A smile pulled at the corners of Adam's lips. So, Marianne had written to him. An apology, no doubt. Well, he was more than willing to be magnanimous, especially when—

"She was hurt," Georgie said, his words effectively destroying Adam's moment of self-congratulation.

"What! What are you saying, lad? Who was hurt? Are you speaking of Miss McCord?"

"Yes, my lord. It was Miss as got hurt. Late last night. I wonder you did not hear her scream. Fair loud enough to wake the dead, it was. Woke me quick enough. At first I thought she was dead, the way she just lay there on the floor, all still like, but Mama said she wasn't dead, only knocked unconscious. Mama chafed her hands until she came around, then later I

held the candle for her when she returned to her bedchamber."

While Georgie told his jumbled story, something resembling a heavy wooden mallet slammed into Adam's chest, hitting him again and again and again, robbing him of breath, and leaving a painful ache where moments before a perfectly healthy heart had resided. He managed through sheer force of will to remain calm, and after realizing that at least two of his servants were listening with unconcealed interest, Adam caught the boy by the shoulder and all but dragged him to the book room.

Once the door was closed behind them, Adam reached out a hand that was far from steady. "Give me the note," he said. After glancing hurriedly at the two sentences, he breathed a sigh of relief, for Marianne's writing appeared lucid enough. Somewhat reassured, Adam instructed the lad to tell him everything that had happened last evening. "And do not leave out a single detail."

Happy to oblige, Georgie told the story from beginning to end, and though he added just a soupçon of little-boy exaggeration to heighten the drama, Adam gained a pretty fair picture of what had occurred. "You are quite certain that Miss McCord was not seriously injured?"

"Yes, sir, I'm certain. It was like my mama predicted, Miss has the headache this morning, but the blow left only a big bump and a bit of a bruise. It didn't bleed even a drop."

Though happy to hear that there was no blood, the lack of it did nothing to stem the tide of Adam's growing rage, not by one iota, and his hands clenched into fists at his side. Only let him ascertain the identity of

the man who dared touch Marianne, and there would be blood aplenty. He promised himself that piece of revenge.

First, though, he had to see her, to assure himself that she was, indeed, recovering.

Opening the book room door, Adam yelled for Sykes, who was surprisingly close at hand.

"Yes, my lord?"

"See that my horse is saddled and brought around. Immediately!"

"Yes, my lord."

To Georgie he said, "Wait here for me, lad, while I change into riding boots. Miss McCord has asked me to call at the grange, and you can ride back with me. You will not mind riding double, I trust, for I am persuaded you will like Mercury."

A big smile split the boy's face. "Yes, sir! I mean, No, sir, I would not mind that at all."

An hour later, her patience exhausted, Marianne decided that Adam was not coming after all. Fortunately, she had only just turned from the window when she heard the *clop, clop, clop* of hoofbeats upon the carriageway. Relief washed over her, and as she stared, unblinking, her face pressed against the glass, she finally spied Adam. Dressed in black top boots, mulberry breeches, and a brown coat, he was astride the large black gelding that had leapt over the trap the day after Marianne arrived at Bibb Grange.

Obviously Adam had not thrown her note into the fire, for he rode quickly, and the moment he reined in the horse, he set Georgie down, then dismounted in one fast yet smooth motion.

"Walk Mercury down the carriageway and back, if you will, lad, while I speak to Miss McCord."

"Yes, my lord."

Not standing on ceremony, Marianne hurried to the entrance door and flung it open before Adam could lift the knocker, a smile of welcome upon her lips. "You came," she said, "I was not certain you would."

He did not answer. He merely stepped across the threshold, then reached his hand out and gently pushed aside the hair that covered the raised place near her left temple. "Are you in pain?" he asked, his voice little more than a whisper.

"Only a very little. My head aches slightly, but nothing to signify."

Adam stared at the bruised flesh, his dark eyes burning with an emotion Marianne could not name. "It signifies," he said, the words cold and tightly controlled.

Her knees had grown weak when Adam touched her, and at his continued scrutiny of her face, Marianne was obliged to battle a totally inappropriate desire to fling herself into his arms and weep all over his chest. Hoping to subdue that urge before it proved victorious, she stepped back, obliging Adam to remove his hand from her head. Feeling suddenly bereft at the loss of contact, she gained control of her wayward emotions by changing the subject.

"As I told you in my note," she said, "I found the second emerald. Or a painting of the pair, to be more precise. There were two stones, each made into a clip suitable for an ornate wig, and unless the artist took some liberty with their likenesses, the gems were very large indeed. Not that I know where the actual stone may be found, of course, but at least we know that it exists."

"Never mind that," Adam said. "At the moment, I am more interested in hearing your description of the intruder. Was it Titus Brougham?"

"I cannot say, not with any degree of certainty, for the corridor was dark, and I did not see the man's face. When I bumped into him, I gained the impression that he was equally startled by the contact. Still, I can attest to the fact that he was a solidly built man, and not much taller than me. And," she added, "though I did not notice the size of his feet, I can tell you that his fingers are short and stubby, and incredibly strong."

"How the deuce do you know about the scoundrel's fingers?"

In answer to his question, Marianne held up her wrist, the one the man had held in his grasp. Five distinct marks showed on her skin, the flesh already turning pinkish-purple.

Adam's indrawn breath was his only response; then, using infinite care, he caught her hand and lifted her wrist to his lips, placing a soft, gentle kiss on each of the five marks. "Better?" he asked.

The feel of his warm lips upon her skin stirred a similar warmth inside Marianne's body, all but liquefying her bones. "Much better," she replied. More than willing to continue this very pleasing therapy, she bid Adam come into the parlor, where they could talk without fear of interruption.

"I cannot," he said. "I have business in the village."

"But you just got here," she said, unable to keep the disappointment from her voice.

"I shall return later."

With that promise she had to be content, for Adam lifted her hand once again, kissed her fingers, then turned and hurried from the house. Like a man on a

mission, he bounded down the three shallow steps and shouted for Georgie, who came running immediately, the gelding trotting happily behind him.

After thanking the boy, Adam threw his leg over the black's back and urged the animal into a gallop. Within a matter of seconds, horse and rider had covered the length of the carriageway, then disappeared around the low stone wall, leaving Marianne standing in the doorway, confused and a bit hurt by Adam's apparent desire to be elsewhere.

Mercury covered the two miles to Chelmford in record time, not slowing even when he crossed the arched bridge. Disapproving of such speed, the swans in the pond trumpeted their outrage, the raucous sound transcending the noise of the water wheel and the ever-present hum of the weaving looms inside the mill.

The village was abustle with activity, probably the result of the previous week of rain, and once Adam crossed the bridge, he was obliged to slow the gelding to a walk to avoid running down a pair of women with baskets of produce over their arms.

After riding past several shops, including one bearing a hand-lettered sign reading WETHINGTON'S, Adam arrived at the small inn that was his destination. He dismounted, handed Mercury's reins over to a young ostler who had come running from the stable, then stepped beneath the swan-shaped sign above the inn door.

He had only just entered the inn, and was waiting for the proprietor, a rotund man in a leather apron, to make his ponderously slow way down the stairs, when Adam was surprised to come face-to-face with a stranger who had just emerged from the taproom. From

the sheepish look on the man's face, he was far from happy to have been caught in that particular spot.

"Lord Jenson!" he said, bowing rather awkwardly. "It's a . . . a pleasure to see you, my lord."

Definitely not a gentleman, the man was in need of a shave, his coat was missing a button, and this was not the first, or even the second day he had worn the same linens. Tall and stockily built, he was no more than forty, and he might have been handsome if time and late morning trips to the pub had not coarsened his features, leaving him with slack jowls and bloodshot eyes.

In no mood to be detained, Adam gave the fellow a look guaranteed to depress pretensions. "Do I know you?"

The man was not so cast away that he did not notice the coolness of Adam's tone, and he stepped back, bowing once again. "Beggin' your lordship's pardon, I'm sure. The name's Bob Quimby. At your service, my lord."

"Quimby? Where have I heard that name before?"

"I manage the mill, my lord."

"Ah, yes, Quimby. I have been meaning to speak with you."

Quimby blinked several times, surprise and growing nervousness making his red eyes protrude like some giant toad's. "Cer-certainly, sir. If your lordship will be so good as to step this way, there's a chair just over there where we can—"

"Not here. What I have to say is best said in private. Be so good as to meet me in your office later this afternoon."

Though couched in polite language, there was no mistaking the lack of cordiality in Adam's tone, and

Bob Quimby's face paled. "Yes, my lord. I shall await your arrival with—"

"Innkeeper!" Adam said, turning his back on Quimby and calling to the rotund man in the apron. "Have you a guest by the name of Titus Brougham?"

"That I do, my lord. I just took a tankard of my best ale up to 'is room. Shall I send word you wish to see 'im, sir?"

"Thank you, no. Merely give me his room number. I should like to surprise him."

"Of course, my lord. Mr. Brougham is in number four, top of the stairs."

Removing a half-guinea from his pocket, Adam placed the gold coin in the innkeeper's outstretched hand and informed him that he and Mr. Brougham did not wish to be disturbed. "No matter what you may hear."

The odd request was not greeted by so much as a raised eyebrow. "I understand perfectly, sir, and I will personally guarantee your lordship's privacy. If you should have need of anything, my lord, you've only to call. Ivers is the name, and I'll be most happy to serve you."

Ignoring the innkeeper's obsequiousness, Adam took the stairs two at a time, then stopped at the door of number four, where he rapped once.

"Go away!" Titus Brougham yelled. "Damnation, Ivers, I told you I did not wish to be disturbed."

Adam opened the door and stepped inside the room. The window hangings were still closed, and the room was in semidarkness, but he had no difficulty in recognizing Titus Brougham's petulant profile. The man sat propped up in the oak full-tester bed, with three or four pillows stacked behind his head and the covers pulled

up to his chest. And though he sipped from the pewter tankard in his hand, his eyes were closed, as though he did not wish to face the day. "Go away," he said again.

"Sorry, Brougham, but my errand cannot wait upon your convenience."

The man jumped, spilling some of the contents of the tankard onto the bedclothes. "Lord Jenson! What the devil do you mean by bursting into my room unannounced?"

Vouchsafing no reply, Adam strode across the room, stopped at the foot of the bed, and leaned his shoulder against the tall oak poster. His manner was relaxed, almost as if this were a social call, but when he spoke, the steel in his voice gave the lie to his posture. "I will ask the questions, Brougham. Were you at Bibb Grange last evening?"

"Bibb Grange? Why . . . why, no, I was not. Though I fail to see what concern that is of yours."

"I have made it my concern."

Titus Brougham did not look at Adam. Instead, he concentrated on placing the tankard on the bedside table to his right. "I was here all evening. In the taproom," he added. "You may ask Ivers if you wish. He will vouch for my presence." Like all liars, Brougham began to embellish in hopes of strengthening his story. "It is a pleasant taproom, and I imbibed a bit unwisely, which explains my reason for remaining abed this morning."

Adam removed a speck of lint from his coat sleeve. "Why is it, I wonder, that I find it so difficult to believe you?"

"I . . . I do not care what you believe!"

"You should, you know."

"Well, I do not. And now, my lord, since you have

asked your question and received your answer, I must insist that you leave me."

The false bravado in the man's voice was not lost on Adam. "Just one more thing," he said.

Giving no warning of his intention, Adam pushed away from the bedpost, his movements so swift they gave Brougham no chance to move away. With all pretense at civility gone, Adam reached out and caught Brougham's right wrist, yanking it toward him so he could examine the man's hand in the dim light. It was as he suspected, the two middle knuckles revealed minor scratches, and the little finger was swollen, as if its owner had hit it against something.

Anger all but choked Adam as he imagined those fleshy fingers balled into a fist and striking Marianne in the temple. "You bastard!"

"Here, now! How dare you speak to me in—"

"Bastard! Maw-worm! What name best suits the kind of low-life coward who would hit a woman?"

Titus Brougham did not answer the question, nor did he continue to pretend he did not understand why Adam was there. Resorting to bravado once again, he said, "If you have come to challenge me to a duel, Jenson, allow me to remind you that they are now illegal. The magistrates do not look favorably upon duelists, and—"

"Challenge you!" Adam could not keep the contempt from his voice. "I do not meet such cowards as you on the field of honor. Men of your ilk I treat like the curs they are."

Having said this, he dragged Brougham from the bed, covers and all.

The man hit the floor with a loud thud. Immediately, he tried to scramble away, but hampered by the twisted counterpane, he found he could not get to his feet. Us-

ing his free hand, he attempted to loosen Adam's fingers. The attempt failed. When he could not free himself from Adam's strong grasp, he began to whimper. "If she had stayed in bed where she belonged, all would have been well. What happened was not my fault!"

"Not your fault? Why, you sniveling—"

"She screamed! What was I to do? I had to stop her before she roused the entire house. Don't you see? I could not help it. It was all the woman's doing. The fault was entirely hers."

Adam dragged the man to the center of the room, then he let go his arm. "Stand up, you dog!"

"I . . . I cannot."

"Stand up," Adam repeated. "Do it! Or I swear, I will thrash you where you lie."

# Twelve

After Adam rode away, Marianne wandered aimlessly through the house. Her emotions were in too much disorder to prompt her to attempt any of the dozens of chores that needed doing, and her head ached too much to allow her to lie down. With no other options, she contented herself with ambling from room to room, wondering every moment why Adam had gone to the village, and more important, when he would return to Bibb Grange.

Unfortunately, walking about did not lessen the throbbing in her temple, and hoping for some relief, Marianne went to the kitchen in search of a cup of strong, sweet tea. When she entered the large, clean room, Hannah was nowhere to be seen, and suspecting the housekeeper might be in the kitchen garden, employed in her daily battle with the weeds, Marianne walked over to the rear door.

Hannah was in the garden right enough, but her battle had nothing to do with weeds. Ben Sims stood several feet away from her, his cap in his hands, and he and Hannah were in the middle of a heated argument.

"You say that again, Ben Sims, and I vow I'll hit you with this hoe."

"Don't be that way, 'Annah. You know I'd never do

ought ter distress you. I like you. I've liked you since I first glimmed eyes on you, only I was too much of a clodpoll to tell you."

Only slightly mollified, Hannah said, "You've a fine way of sweet-talking a girl. Repeating gossip you know'll rile her."

"I b'aint no gossiper," he said, "and I take no joy in repeating what the whole village is saying. I just thought you'd rather 'ear it from me, is all."

"You thought I would want to hear lies about Miss McCord?"

At the sound of her name, Marianne stiffened.

"It b'aint lies, 'Annah. The story come from a gentleman what knows it ter be true. 'E says 'e's got proof."

"Gentleman or no, he's lying if he says miss is a bast—that she's somebody's natural daughter."

Marianne felt as if she had been turned to stone, and for just a moment she was nine years old again, standing outside the village church, eavesdropping on one of the local children and a visitor, the prettiest girl Marianne had ever seen.

The little girl was about Marianne's age, and she had long, blond ringlets and sky-blue eyes. Her face was that of an angel, and Marianne was convinced that she and that beautiful child were destined to be friends for life. Afraid to approach her, but even more afraid to let the opportunity pass her by, Marianne had taken a deep breath, crossed her fingers for luck, then walked over to the two girls. "Hello," she said to the angel. "My name is Marianne."

"I know who you are," the angel replied. "And I know *what* you are, only it is a naughty word, and if I say it, Nurse will wash my mouth with soap."

Marianne knew the word the child meant; she had been called it often enough before.

"Go home," the other little girl said.

"Yes," the angel agreed, "get away from us. My mother says I am not to speak to you."

Marianne had left the two girls, of course, what else could she do, but only when she was far away from the churchyard did she let the tears fall. She had been mocked and teased before, and it had always hurt her, but it had been so much more painful to be spurned by an angel.

Now, here she was, all grown up, and it was happening again. And this time the pain in her chest was almost unbearable. It ached as though someone had forcibly removed her heart. The angel had spurned her, but this was much worse. This was betrayal.

Only one person in Chelmford could have started the rumor about her illegitimacy, for Marianne had trusted only one person with that particular secret. She had told no one the story but Adam Jenson.

*Adam!* Just thinking his name made her want to cry out in anguish. She loved Adam—in the entire world, he was the only person she loved—and he had betrayed her. Why? How could he have done it?

True, she had made him angry—insulted him, perhaps, about the closing of the school and his obligation to the villagers. Was this Adam's method of revenge? To tell everyone about her birth? She had not thought him capable of duplicity, but what else was she to think? What other *gentleman* could have done it?

She did not cry. She could not. The blessed relief of tears was denied her, for she had cried too many times in her life. This time the hurt was too great; the tears would not come.

Less than an hour later, when Adam returned to the grange, Marianne was in her bedchamber, the door locked.

"Miss," Hannah said after knocking softly. "Lord Jenson is here, and he asked if you would see him."

Marianne did not open the door.

All the things she had wanted to say to Adam—all the clever, vindictive words she had rehearsed in the past hour so she would have them ready to throw at him—vanished from her thoughts. All she could think of was how much she loved him. How much she would always love him. She wanted to go to him, and yet, the pain of his betrayal was too new, too raw, like an ache that radiated throughout her entire body, rendering her numb and incapable of taking even one step toward the door.

"Tell his lordship that I cannot see him."

"But, miss, his face is—"

"Tell him I am indisposed."

The housekeeper did not argue but went belowstairs to deliver the message. A few minutes later, Marianne heard diminishing hoofbeats on the carriageway and knew that Adam had ridden away. The sound was almost her undoing, for she felt tears sting her eyes.

"Oh, no!" she said, her voice quivering with combined anger and pain. "You will not cry now, Marianne McCord. Not now!"

"Miss," Hannah said, once again outside the bedchamber door, "Lord Jenson left a message."

Marianne said nothing.

"His lordship said he had business at the mill this afternoon, but he would be back later to see how you got on. And he said he hoped you had a good rest."

*And I hope he falls in the mill pond and drowns!*

No. She did not mean that. She did not want any harm to come to Adam. She just wanted him out of her life, and she wanted out of his life as well. Of course, there had never been a real place in his life for her anyway. A wealthy viscount and a female born on the wrong side of the blanket? And one who would be twenty-six in two days! An old maid. With no hope of ever finding happiness.

Not that she ever could be happy with anyone but Adam. No matter what he had done, Marianne's heart belonged to him and him alone. She would never love another.

"And that, too, is your fault, Adam Jenson. You have ruined any chance I might have had to fall in love with some other man. Some man who might have understood about my parentage and loved me in spite of it."

No, she would never love again. As Vince Sims had told his son, only a fool makes the same mistake twice.

Her anger revived, strengthened by the suspicion that she had already been a fool, Marianne strode over to the Queen Anne desk, her intention to write Adam a letter telling him not to return to Bibb Grange, that she never wanted to see him again. Not ever!

To add fuel to the fire of her anger, she discovered that all the vellum was gone. She had used the last of the stack to bid Adam come to her the evening before. Now she had none left to bid him stay away.

"There must be another piece of paper somewhere!"

With her frustration growing, Marianne tried to force open the shallow drawer that had not budged the other dozen times she had tried to force it. This time, however, she was in no mood to be gainsaid. She would open that drawer now—this minute—or know the reason why!

After hitting the front several times with her hand and even crawling beneath the desk to kick the underside with her foot—all without success—Marianne made up her mind to pry open the drawer. With that objective in mind, she stormed down to the kitchen, found Hannah's thick steel butcher knife, then returned to the bedchamber.

Once Marianne had forced the tip of the broad steel into the minuscule space between the top of the drawer and the strong casework that held it in place, she twisted the blade, not caring that it splintered the lovely old walnut, only that it accomplished the job. It needed only two twists of the knife before the drawer gave way.

"And now," she said as though the desk could hear, "let me see what has been keeping you—"

The words, as well as Marianne's anger, died instantly, for the obstruction proved to be a thick stack of letters, perhaps twenty or more, all tied together with a man's black silk shoelace. The pages were yellowed with age but not so discolored that Marianne did not recognize the neat copperplate on the topmost letter. The handwriting was that of Daisy McCord, Marianne's mother.

With trembling fingers, Marianne untied the silk that secured the stack. Her mother's letter was directed to Lieutenant Marcus Wilson, in care of Mr. Theodore Bibb, Bibb Grange, Chelmsford, Derbyshire. For a moment, Marianne could only stare, amazed to discover that her mother had known Mr. Bibb after all—or if not the man, at least his direction. But what connection did he have with Marcus Wilson, Marianne's father?

The seal securing the cover page of her mother's letter

had never been broken. Marianne broke it now, unfolded the pages, and read the closely written lines.

*My beloved husband,*

*I am sending this letter care of your mother's brother because I believe my father has done something to prevent the letters I sent to your barracks from ever reaching you. I know if you had received my letters, you would have come to me, as I begged you to do, and taken me away with you.*

*Let my father say what he will about having our marriage put aside, in my heart I am your wife— now and forever—and nothing Father can do will change the way I feel. Only tell me where I may come to be with you, and I will come there. Nothing can keep us apart, my love. Nothing.*

*Your adoring wife,*
*Daisy Wilson*

The two dozen letters that completed the stack were directed to Mr. Theodore Bibb as well. Though they were all written in a hand unfamiliar to Marianne, she knew even before she read the first letter that they had been written by Marcus Wilson. As she skimmed through those letters, which spanned seventeen years, she found nothing personal, only comments about military life and the occasional bit of news regarding the writer's promotions from lieutenant all the way to major.

Still, Marianne's hands quivered like an aspen, for those pages had been held by her father, the words written in his own hand. It was the final letter, however, that caused the tears to well in her eyes, then course down her cheeks, for the letter was dated 1809, in the very month her mother had died.

*Dear Uncle,*

*By now you will have heard of the battle fought at Vimiero, in the Peninsula. Had you been here, you would have been proud of Wellesley and all the brave lads who fought at his side. I like to think, Uncle, that you would have been proud of me as well.*

*As my only living relative save my cousin Titus, who has neither my affection nor my respect, I ask you to do one favor for me.*

*Seventeen years ago, I was married—am still married in my heart—and though the young lady's father had the marriage put aside, I have never stopped loving her. I have written to Daisy many times over the years, but my letters have never been answered.*

*I am sorry to be the one to tell you this, Uncle, but I am wounded, and the surgeon informs me that I will not recover. It is my dying wish that you let my beloved wife know of my demise.*

*Also, though I would have liked to say these words to her myself, will you tell Daisy that no day goes by that I do not think of her, and that with my last breath I will speak her name.*

*Thank you, Uncle. I can rest easy now, knowing that you will fulfill my last request. I am, as always,*

*Your loving nephew,*
*Marcus*

Marianne let the letter fall from her hand, for she could no longer see for the flood of tears. Her father had loved her mother to the end, just as Daisy had loved him, and the two had died within days of each other.

After a time, when the tears had abated somewhat,

Marianne searched through the shallow drawer for further letters. There was only one more, and this was from Mr. J. Penell, Mr. Theodore Bibb's solicitor.

*Dear Sir,*

*I am happy to inform you that I have discovered the whereabouts of Miss Daisy McCord—Mrs. Marcus Wilson, actually, for the marriage was never put aside.*

*If you would like me to do so, I can inform the lady of her husband's demise. If that is not your wish, let me know.*

*I have enclosed Mrs. Wilson's address, should you wish to contact her yourself.*

*Yr. Obd. Serv.*
*J. Penell, Esq.*

Marianne read the lawyer's letter through twice, then she set it on the desk and bent to retrieve the letter she had dropped, the final one from her father—from her mother's husband.

They were married. Her parents were married all those years. Her grandfather had never followed through on his threat, though he had been mean-spirited enough to keep the couple apart and to let his daughter believe she had borne a child out of wedlock. Marianne might never know the extent of the unscrupulous things Hyram McCord had done, but it was obvious that he had somehow intercepted his daughter's letters, correspondence both to and from her young husband.

And he had told his daughter that the man she loved was dead years before it was true!

Poor Daisy. Poor Marcus. Two lives ruined because of an old man's pride and arrogance.

"But not three lives!" she said, rising from the desk chair. "You have not ruined my life, you cruel old martinet, and I do not mean to suffer ever again from the stigma you allowed to be placed upon me."

With a speed increased by purpose, Marianne donned a hat and gathered her reticule, then, after reclaiming the solicitor's letter, she sped down the steps and into the kitchen, calling Hannah's name as she ran.

"Sorry, miss," Georgie said, "but Mama just left. She's driving the trap into the village to fetch supplies."

"With Bess?" A foolish question, of course with Bess, for they had no other horse. "How long ago did they leave?"

"Two minutes. Maybe less."

Without another word, Marianne turned and sped through the house, exiting the front door without sparing time to close it. Knowing Bess, there was every chance Marianne could outrun the mare and catch up with the trap somewhere in the lane. As luck would have it, she caught them just before they passed through the low stone wall.

"Hannah! Wait!"

Hannah reined in the mare, but before she could ask what was amiss, Marianne had climbed aboard the trap and taken the reins from the housekeeper's hands.

"Go, Bess," Marianne called to the mare, "move as you have never moved before. I have business in the village, business that will not wait, for I have a letter to show a certain viscount."

Naturally, Bess took no interest in the vagaries of humans and refused to alter her usual speed by so much as a second; therefore, Marianne was obliged to exercise at least a degree of patience. She was unable to keep her news to herself, however, so as they traveled the

two miles to Chelmford, she told Hannah of her discovery.

"I'm that happy for you, miss, that you found the letter from the solicitor, but why must you show it to the viscount this very minute? You've had an injury, and you should be back at the grange, lying on your bed, regaining your strength. Besides, if I know aught of the matter, that letter will make no difference to his lordship."

"What do you mean?"

"Beggin' your pardon if I'm speaking out of turn, miss, but I don't think it would matter to Lord Jenson if you were the daughter of the Tyburn hangman himself, not the way his lordship feels about you."

"He feels nothing for me, otherwise he would not have started the rumor in the village."

Hannah turned to stare at her, suspicion in her glance. "And what rumor would that be, miss?"

"You know the one I mean." Marianne had the grace to blush. "Your pardon for eavesdropping, Hannah, but I could not help hearing Ben tell you that a gentleman had spread it about the village that I was someone's natural daughter."

When Hannah spoke, her voice was noticeably cool. "If you could not help hearing the first part, miss, you should have stayed long enough to hear the whole. The gentleman Ben mentioned was not his lordship, but someone who is staying at the inn."

Marianne felt stunned, as though she had been hit by a bolt of lightning. "Not the viscount?"

"No, miss."

"But, I . . . that is, he knew about me. I told him, believing he would honor my confidence."

"Which he did."

When Marianne said nothing, could not have spoken if her life had depended upon it, Hannah continued. "How could you think that his lordship would betray you? You must know how much he admires you. Why, when a gentleman fights for a lady, it's a sure sign he—"

"Fights! What do you mean?"

"When he came to see you this afternoon, after his trip to the village, there was a cut at the side of his lip—a cut that did not get there when his lordship was shaving."

"But that does not mean he was fighting, and for me. Surely you are mistaken."

"I've a brother and a son," Hannah said, impatience showing in her voice, "I know when a cut comes from a blow aimed by a fist."

"But—"

"If anyone was to ask me how his lordship came by that cut, I'd stake my Sunday bonnet that he found the man who hit you last evening, and he gave the scoundrel what-for."

Though the sky was a clear blue, Marianne felt the jolt of a second lightning bolt. So many times in her childhood days she had longed for someone to take her part, and now someone had done so. Adam had fought for her, had even been wounded, and all the time she had been pitching a temper tantrum, believing him to have betrayed her!

"Oh, Hannah. I have acted like a fool."

"Yes, miss. Women in love often do."

Nothing more was said, for Bess had approached the mill pond, and though the mare had never before refused to cross the stone bridge, this time she would not put so much as a hoof on it. Marianne flicked the reins to encourage the animal, then she alternately cajoled and

threatened. The mare would not budge. Instead, she tossed her head, her nostrils flared, and her eyes rolled back as if in fear.

"What ails the animal?"

Hannah did not hear the question, for she was staring toward the mill office, where a man was peering into one of the windows, his actions decidedly suspicious-looking. She gasped. "That man," she said, her voice hushed. "He looks like—" Her hand went to her throat. "It's him!"

"Him, who?"

Marianne looked at the man who had left the window and was now skulking away from the building as if he did not want to be seen.

"It's the gentleman I told you about. Georgie's father."

"What! Are you certain?"

"He's changed in twelve years. He's plumper and not nearly so handsome as he was, 'specially not with his face all bruised and swollen, but it's him all right—the one as took advantage of me."

"Took advantage! Hannah, I thought— That is, you never said—"

"What was the point? What's the word of a mill worker's daughter against that of a gentleman? It's the way of the world, miss. To tell would only have made matters worse. Besides, I didn't even know his name. Still don't."

"Titus Brougham," Marianne said. "The scoundrel is Mr. Bibb's nephew, Titus Brougham."

Thinking to overtake the man and give him a piece of her mind, Marianne urged Bess to continue across the bridge. Once again, the mare refused, and this time she whinnied and began to back away.

"What on earth has gotten into that mare? She's acting as though—"

"It's smoke," Hannah said, sniffing the air.

Marianne sniffed as well, and as she did so, alarm prickled at her spine, for there was a definite hint of smoke in the air, the acrid smell unmistakable. But where was it coming from?

"Heaven help us," Hannah yelled. She pointed toward the redbrick mill. "The manager's office is afire!"

# Thirteen

*Fire!*

The word struck fear in Marianne's heart, and like the mare, her first instinct was to back away, to flee from danger. She could not do so, however, for unlike Bess, Marianne knew that several hundred people were inside the mill. If the fire in the office spread, the workers in the mill itself would be in jeopardy.

And what of Adam? Was he still in the office?

Marianne's first instinct was to run to the office, screaming Adam's name, but something told her that if she did so, she might cause panic inside the mill. Recalling tales of a workhouse fire in London during the previous century, she knew that panic in a crowded building could cause deaths more quickly than the fire itself.

"The volunteer fire brigade," Hannah said. "I'll run to the village and get them."

"Excellent. While you get help, I will go to the mill office to make certain the manager and Adam have finished with their meeting and are no longer inside."

The two women scrambled down from the trap, then hurried to do their chosen tasks. Meanwhile, Bess, free from constraint, turned and fled toward home, moving faster than a colt, the trap bumping and jolting behind

her. The swans on the mill pond had obviously smelled
the smoke as well, for they set up a series of shrill
trumpetings and swam as far as possible in the other
direction.

Marianne was so frightened, her knees threatened to
give way beneath her, but she walked at a brisk pace
toward the mill office, not stopping until she arrived at
the window where she had seen Titus Brougham looking
in. She had to stand on tiptoe to see inside.

At first she thought the small, cramped room was
empty, for she saw no one sitting behind the square,
utilitarian desk or in the wooden visitor's chair opposite
the desk. When she looked more closely, however, she
spied a pair of gentleman's top boots lying on their
sides, sticking out from behind the legs of the chair.

Her heart began to hammer in her chest, for the boots
contained feet, and Marianne could see a bit of mulberry cloth above the turned-back tops. Adam had worn
mulberry breeches when he visited her earlier, she recalled.

But why was he on the floor? And why had he not
fled at the first sign of smoke?

At this close range, Marianne could see the smoke
she had only smelled before. It swirled inside the small
office, appearing thickest close to the ceiling, but with
each second it grew ever thicker and ever closer to the
floor. Gray-white, it looked harmless enough, but Marianne knew the benign look was an illusion.

Smoke was an insidious killer, silent as a snake and
many times more dangerous. Not only did it affect visi-
bility, concealing escape routes, but it would also render
a person unconscious in a matter of minutes—life-steal-
ing minutes that left a person to perish in the heat of
the encroaching flames.

Had Adam succumbed to the smoke and passed out? It seemed early for that to have happened, for there was still breathable air close to the floor. Whatever the truth, Marianne knew she must do something, or the man she loved would perish.

The door to the office was around at the side of the building, and when Marianne reached it, she found it padlocked. Someone had forced the barrel of a pocket pistol through the link, effectively imprisoning anyone unfortunate enough to be inside the building.

For luck, Marianne touched the golden acorn at her neck, but at the same time she prayed for help from above. "Please," she begged, "do not let anything happen to Adam."

The wooden door was warm to the touch, and many times while Marianne struggled to work the pistol barrel free of the lock, she was obliged to cough, for the smoke was growing thicker. At last, with one determined yank, she managed to pull the pistol out of the padlock. To her horror, she discovered that both shots had been discharged, and as she tossed the useless weapon on the ground, she added a second prayer that Adam was not already dead.

When she threw open the door, the outside air rushed inside, causing a *whooshing* sound, and immediately flames sprung up in the corner of the office, where piles of papers had been tossed, then set afire. Like red and orange dancers of death, the flames leapt from the papers to the sleeve of a coat that hung on a nearby coat tree.

Grabbing at her skirt, Marianne yanked the hem of the garment up to cover her mouth and nose, then she entered the small room. Keeping close to the ground,

where the air was clearer, she went straight to the place she had seen the top boots.

The boots belonged to Adam right enough; he lay on the floor, his arms akimbo, as if he had fallen. He did not move. A trickle of blood stained his forehead, the culprit a bullet, presumably from the discarded pistol. Fortunately, the bullet had only grazed the skin, knocking Adam unconscious. The other man, whom Marianne supposed must be Bob Quimby, had not been so lucky.

The mill manager was in the opposite corner, half sitting half lying on the floor, his face slack and his eyes open in a permanent stare. A reddish-brown stain had spread large and ominous-looking on the front of his shirt, its core just above his heart. If there was any help for Bob Quimby, it was in the hereafter. For now, Marianne must see to the man who still clung to this world.

After pushing the chair aside, she got down on her knees beside the man she loved, speaking directly into his ear. "Adam, please wake up. We must get out of here."

His only response was a moan, followed by a paroxysm of coughing. *Thank God!* If he could still cough, there was hope he might regain consciousness.

She grabbed his arm and shook it as hard as she could "Adam! Adam!"

He moaned again, then he opened his eyes and blinked, staring at her as if he thought he might be dreaming. "Wha-what is it?"

"You must get up!" she shouted, then shook his arm again.

"Ouch! That hurts. Blast it all, stop shak—" The final word was lost in another bout of coughing. When the

paroxysm subsided, Adam appeared spent, and he leaned his head back, resting it against her bent knee.

Frustrated and more frightened than she had ever been in her entire life, Marianne made a fist and hit him on the shoulder. "I said get up! Adam, do you hear me? Open your eyes and get up off this floor! I will not let you remain here to die."

When he did not open his eyes, Marianne stood, took his booted feet, one beneath each of her arms, and began dragging him inch by inch toward the door. He was a large man, tall and muscular, and the task of pulling him across the wooden floor was almost beyond her strength. At one time, she was so overcome by smoke that she was forced to stumble outside to gulp clean, fresh air into her lungs.

Her throat and chest hurt, and the skin on her face and arms felt hot and painfully tight. The temptation was great to fall to the soft, damp grass and stay there, not to return to that hellish place where fear and death awaited her, but she knew she could not remain outside, not while Adam was within. "I will not leave him in there," she said, "I love him too much."

In an instant, she was back inside the smoke-filled office, catching Adam's legs again and tugging them with all her might. The whole of the back and side walls were now engulfed in flames, and the fire had licked its way up to the ceiling. Marianne knew that if she did not get Adam out within the next minute, the ceiling would collapse, trapping both of them.

"Please, God," she said, "help me do this."

From somewhere came the strength for one last, impossible tug, and the next thing Marianne knew, she was lying on the damp grass again, coughing and gasping for air.

Adam lay on the ground beside her. His face and neck were black with ash, and he lay still as death. For one frightening moment, Marianne's world came to an end, for she thought he had succumbed to the smoke. Then, in one, sudden, convulsive movement, her beloved pitched over onto his stomach and began to retch.

If anyone had told Marianne McCord five days earlier that she would soon be obliged to turn visitors and well-wishers away from her door, she would not have believed them. Such was the case, however, and when Hannah brought another vase of flowers up to the master bedchamber, Marianne claimed fatigue and bid her send the caller away.

"I am too tired to see anyone else today. Thank whoever brought the bouquet, and please express my appreciation to those villagers who brought the jams and seed cakes, but tell them I must get some rest. And whatever else you do," she added, pointing to a ball of yellow fur at the foot of the bed, "take that blasted cat away! She has taken root there and watches every move I make, as though she is standing guard."

Hannah set the vase of hothouse roses and chrysanthemums on the bedside table, then she scooped Butterball from the foot of the bed and settled the cat beneath her arm. "I'll do as you wish, miss, and send everyone away. Though if I know ought of the matter, I think you will want to speak with the gentleman who brought the flowers."

*Gentleman! Had Adam come at last?*

Her fatigue miraculously gone, Marianne sat up quickly, plumping the pillows behind her back and

straightening the lace-edged pink bed shawl Miss Faye Havor had brought her only that morning.

Marianne understood why Adam had not come to see her those first few days, for like her, he needed bed rest and time for his injured lungs to heal. But that time was passed now, and since sunrise that morning she had spent every minute listening for him . . . waiting, hoping, longing to see him.

Never mind. He was here at last, and that was all that mattered. With a wide, possibly foolish smile upon her face, she bid Hannah show the gentleman up.

The smile died a quick death when a middle-aged man she had never seen before stepped into the room and made her a businesslike bow. "Miss McCord," he said, "permit me to extend to you my felicitations upon your fortunate recovery, and my most heartfelt congratulations upon your unbelievably courageous rescue of Viscount Jenson. I spoke with the doctor his lordship sent round to see to your care, and the good doctor assures me that your recuperation will be swift and complete."

Too disappointed to exercise tact, Marianne said, "Who are you?"

The gray-haired gentleman bowed again. "How remiss of me. I am J. Throckmorton Penell, the late Mr. Bibb's solicitor. I had meant to call upon you when you first took up residence at Bibb Grange, to explain certain portions of Mr. Bibb's last will and testament—portions best not discussed in a letter. Unfortunately, pressing business matters detained me in London, until now."

Mr. Penell walked over to the window, giving his attention to the scenery as though embarrassed by what he was about to say. "Miss McCord," he began, "I must

apologize for my carelessness when Titus Brougham called upon me shortly after his uncle's demise."

Interested in spite of her previous disappointment, Marianne gave him her full attention. "Carelessness?" she repeated.

The solicitor nodded, then he turned to look at her straight on. "When Mr. Brougham came to see me, inquiring about the possible whereabouts of an emerald he seemed to think was part of Mr. Bibb's estate, certain papers were on my desk. Those papers, and the information they contained, came to me by way of a Bow Street Runner I had hired several months earlier to locate your mother and to find out all he could about her situation. Naturally, the runner included in his report the quite unfounded belief held by those who knew you and your mother that your birth was . . . was—"

"I understand, sir. You need not distress yourself by speaking the words."

"You are very gracious, ma'am."

She waved aside his polite murmurings. "Pray, continue with your story, Mr. Penell."

"I make no excuses for my negligence, Miss McCord, for I should not have left those papers on my desk when I stepped outside to speak to my clerk. Still, I wanted you to know that Mr. Brougham looked through the papers without my consent. It was a thoroughly reprehensible act and one I would never have expected from a gentleman."

"Mr. Brougham is no gentleman."

"As you say, ma'am. There can be but one opinion on the subject. As well, after hearing all the fellow has done while here in Derbyshire, I begin to think Titus Brougham is deranged. I should have guessed it from

the way he refused to believe there was no second emerald."

"Oh? Is there not? In the painting," she said, pointing to the portrait of the mother with her children, "the lady is wearing two hair clips."

He did not even bother to look at the painting. "There were two clips, to be sure, ma'am. One was the original emerald, the other a paste copy."

The solicitor straightened his cravat as though uncomfortable to be revealing facts about his clients, even those long deceased. "Mr. Theodore Bibb's father, though an East India Company nabob, was not as wealthy as many people believed him to be. When the second of his twin daughters married, becoming Mrs. Augusta Brougham, the nabob included the emerald as part of his daughter's dowry. Though I have no way of knowing for certain, it is possible that the paste copy was given as a keepsake to Mrs. Aurelia Wilson, your paternal grandmother. The only value to the copy was purely sentimental, so it may have been discarded years ago."

Mr. Penell cleared his throat. "I hope, ma'am, that you are not too disappointed about the gem."

"No, not at all. Even if it existed, and I had found it, I would not have considered it to be mine."

"Actually, if such a gem had existed, it would have been yours without question. Mr. Theodore Bibb did not approve of Titus Brougham, whom he considered a wastrel. On the other hand, he was quite fond of his other nephew, Major Marcus Wilson, who led an exemplary life. For that reason, Bibb Grange—everything in the house and on the estate—was left to Major Wilson, and upon his demise, to Major Wilson's wife. Everything. No exceptions. Therefore, if there had been a sec-

ond emerald on the premises, it would have belonged
to your mother and then to you."

"And that is what Titus Brougham believed? That his
uncle had hidden the emerald here in the house?"

Mr. Penell nodded. "Yes, I think he must have. He
was in desperate need of money, and desperate men
often allow themselves to be deluded."

"That would explain why he felt obliged to break
into the house—to steal the gem before I accidentally
found it."

"As to his attempt to steal the stone, and his subse-
quent attack upon your person, there is no explaining
such behavior. As I said before, he must be deranged."

"Speaking of Mr. Brougham, do you know if he has
been found?"

"Not to my knowledge, ma'am. Although I understand that Bow Street has put a dozen of their best men
on the case. If Brougham is fortunate, the runners will
find him and bring him to trial. Otherwise, he might
be apprehended by the man to whom he owes several
thousand pounds in gaming debts, in which instance, he
would probably forfeit his life."

"His is not a hopeful future."

"No, ma'am, it is not. In any event, you need have
no fear, for Brougham is not crazy enough to ever come
back here. Not with the entire village ready to murder
him on sight."

"Do you blame them?"

Mr. Penell shook his head. "I do not, ma'am, for by
setting that fire to wreak vengeance on Lord Jenson,
Titus Brougham risked the lives of half the people in
Chelmford. Just as you and your housekeeper, by your
quick thinking and courage, saved the mill and the
workers inside the building."

The last thing Marianne wanted to discuss was her part in the rescue, but she very much wanted to ask about Adam. Trying for a nonchalant tone, she said, "You mentioned Lord Jenson. Sir, have you, perchance, spoken to him since you arrived?"

"Why, no, ma'am. I called upon him, of course, I thought it only proper that I do so, but he was not at home."

Surprised, Marianne said, "But I thought he must still be abed, nursing his injuries. Otherwise, why has he not come to—" She stopped abruptly, for she very nearly asked why Adam had not been to see her.

"Still abed?" The solicitor laughed as though she had made a jest. "Not the viscount. Gentlemen such as he—Corinthians and athletes of the first order—do not pamper themselves."

Weary of tiptoeing around the question she most wanted to ask, Marianne said, "If he is not at Jenson Hall, then, where is he?"

"According to Mr. Sykes, his lordship's butler, Lord Jenson and his friend, Mr. Franklin Llewellyn, have returned to London."

# Fourteen

Marianne's birthday arrived, and she did not even bother to tell anyone. What was the point? It was just another day, and lately one day seemed pretty much like the one before it, dull and without purpose.

Still, she knew she must get on with her life, and she had determined to do so. In fact, each morning she vowed anew to stop moping around like some lovesick schoolgirl and become involved in the activities of the village. The only problem was that with Adam gone from Derbyshire, life seemed to have lost its flavor.

True, she no longer figured as the village scandal, and she had even received a dinner invitation from Sir Percival and Lady Havor, and an invitation to tea from the vicar's wife, but those offers of friendship brought her little joy. The person she wished to dine with was Adam Jenson, and she wished to take tea with him and him alone.

Unfortunately, it seemed those two wishes would never be granted, for Adam had returned to his old life in London. His original purpose in coming to Chelmford had been to recuperate from the gunshot wound to his side. With that wound now completely healed, there was nothing to keep him in Derbyshire. Nothing.

It was a lowering thought but one Marianne had told

herself repeatedly she must accept. She had known from the very beginning of their friendship that she and Adam were from two different worlds, but at that time she had not known that she would one day love him with all her heart, or that her heart would ache without ceasing once he was no longer in her life.

It had been two weeks since Adam and his friend had left Jenson Hall, and though Faye Havor had shared with Marianne a note she received from Mr. Llewellyn, expressing his intention of returning to Chelmford in the very near future, there had been no word at all from Adam. At least, none to Marianne.

Therefore, it was with great surprise that the melancholy lady, returning from a walk about the grounds on the morning of her birthday, discovered a lovely little chestnut mare with golden mane and tail pawing the ground outside the entrance to her home. Another horse, ridden by one of the Jenson Hall grooms, stood beside the mare.

"Ma'am," the groom said, touching the bill of his cap, "I was told ter bring this 'ere mare around for you."

"For me? I do not understand. Who sent it? And why?"

"All's I know, miss, is what I'm told. I'm ter ask if you're still willing ter play chaperone for an owl fresky nuncheon."

"Oh," she said, her heart beating madly. Afraid to hope that Adam had returned to the Hall, she asked, "Has . . . er, Mr. Llewellyn come for another stay?"

"That 'e 'as, miss. As we speak, the gentleman is on 'is way ter fetch Miss 'Avor, and if you're still agreeable ter chaperone, I'm ter escort you ter the knoll on t'other side of the village."

For one brief moment, Marianne had felt alive again, but with the information that it was Mr. Llewellyn and not Adam who had sent the horse, the gloom that had weighed upon her for more than a fortnight returned. Nevertheless, she had given her promise to chaperone Faye, who seemed sincerely attached to Mr. Llewellyn, and she would not go back on her word.

"I must change," she said, indicating the green sprigged muslin she had worn for her walk. "Give me fifteen minutes, and I will join you here."

"Yes, miss."

Faithful to her promise, Marianne opened the door fifteen minutes later, ready to go. Hannah had helped her dress, and though the housekeeper had admired the dark blue velvet habit and the little blue hat with the jaunty feather that touched Marianne's shoulder, the lady knew the ensemble was ten years or more out of fashion. Still, it gave her a bit of a lift to receive the sincere compliment.

Her spirits were buoyed as well by the pleasure of being in the saddle once again. The little chestnut was a sweetheart, with a soft mouth and a lively manner, and since it had not rained for more than a week, the ground was perfect for riding. As well, the day was warm and beautiful, with the sky so blue it rivaled the forget-me-nots that grew around the mill pond.

As she and the groom crossed over the bridge and passed by the pond, Marianne sighed, for if Adam had been waiting for her at the knoll on such a wonderful day, life would have been perfect. "Ingrate," she muttered, "enjoy the beauty around you and stop wishing for things that can never be."

Within five minutes, the mill and the shops and cottages of the village were behind them, with the rolling

green knoll just up ahead. A large stand of late-bloom-
ing white hawthorn bushes grew to the side of the knoll,
and quite near the bushes Faye Havor's groom, Jem,
waited. The middle-aged man held the reins of his own
and two other horses, one of them the gray Faye preferred. Several feet away stood a handsome curricle and
pair.

Though Marianne wondered to whom the equipage
belonged, she heard laughter from somewhere on the
other side of the knoll and immediately put the question
from her mind. Perhaps Mr. Llewellyn had brought a
friend with him.

"Very funny, old boy," Mr. Llewellyn said, "now tell
the lady how you got the bullet in the first place."

"What! And sully Miss Havor's ears with stories of
my sordid past?"

At the sound of that deep, melodious voice Marianne's breath caught in her throat. *Oh, please. Let me
not be imagining it.*

"Ah" Adam continued, turning to watch Marianne as
she reached the top of the knoll, "unless my eyes de-
ceive me, here is the girl with the red riding cape. If
she is so inclined, she can tell Miss Havor all about the
big bad wolf, for she knows him better than most. I
believe she even calls him friend."

"Is that so, Miss McCord?" Faye Havor asked.

Marianne did not answer. She had eyes and ears for
no one but Adam. Since he was walking toward her at
that moment, his hands outstretched to receive hers, an
Atlantic gale could have hit the knoll and Marianne
would not have noticed.

When last she saw Adam, his skin and hair were covered in ash and he smelled of charred wood. Now, however, he was the picture of health: tall and vibrant, his

thick black hair a bit longer than was his usual style, but his near-black eyes were just the same, alive and warm and completely mesmerizing.

He was undoubtedly the most beautiful man Marianne had ever seen, and she loved him so much, it frightened her.

"Hello," he said.

"Adam," she replied, the word little more than a whisper. She placed her hands in his, and at his touch, all Marianne's previous melancholy fell away. Like the day, life was beautiful again. Adam was here.

"Forgive me for sending the groom to fetch you," he said. "I wanted to come myself, but I had business in the village. The new mill manager returned with us from London, and I felt it my duty to introduce him to the master weavers."

"Of course."

Marianne was very much afraid she would have forgiven Adam anything, just as long as he did not let go of her hands. With him close to her, and smiling down at her once more, her heart had awakened with a vengeance, pumping at double time, and all was forgotten save the joy of being with the man she loved.

"You went away," she said, not caring one whit that Mr. Llewellyn and Miss Havor might hear the longing in her voice. "And I feared you meant never to return."

"What! And miss seeing the kittens grow up? How could you think it?"

Though his words were teasing, the serious look in those dark eyes gave Marianne reason to hope that he had *other* reasons for returning.

Her silent prayer for a moment alone with Adam was answered when Mr. Llewellyn made some excuse about walking Miss Havor over to the hawthorn bushes to pick

a bouquet for the nuncheon. "We shan't be above five minutes," he said.

"Take your time," Adam replied. "I have something I should like to say to Marianne."

"You do?" she asked, feeling quite breathless.

"How can you doubt it? Even a rag-mannered fellow like me knows enough to thank a lady for saving his life."

"Oh, that," she said, disappointment in her voice.

"Yes, *that,* my brave girl."

"I beg of you, do not give it another thought, for I was not brave in the least. If the truth be known, I was so frightened, my knees kept threatening to buckle beneath me."

"Yet you entered a burning building and pulled me out to safety. How you managed it, I do not know, a slip of a girl like you. If I should live to be a hundred, I shall never cease to admire your courage."

"Please, I wish you would not, for I did only what had to be done. And I promise you, I was scared witless."

"Which is the epitome of bravery, my sweet love, for you did the very thing you needed to be brave about."

"What? What did you say?"

"I said that bravery is—"

"No, no. That other thing. What did you call me?"

Adam smiled, and as he did so, he tugged at her hands, obliging her to move closer to him, so they were mere inches apart. "I called you my sweet love. For that is what you are, you know. Surely you must have guessed how much I love you."

Marianne shook her head. She wanted to believe that he loved her, oh, how she wanted to believe it, but she could not bear it if his feelings were nothing more than

gratitude to her for saving his life. "Adam, if this is some misguided feeling on your part—"

"It is most definitely misguided, my sweet, for an innocent like you has no business even entertaining a proposal from a man like me."

Marianne was obliged to swallow to relieve the tightness in her throat. "A proposal? You cannot mean a proposal of marriage?"

"I was afraid you would not take me seriously, so I took the precaution of journeying to Kent to fetch the family betrothal ring."

He let go of her hand long enough to reach inside the watch pocket of his waistcoat. "It is a pretty thing," he said, withdrawing a gold ring containing a large sapphire encircled by diamonds. "Unfortunately, it is nowhere near as lovely as you."

This was all happening too fast. Marianne had dreamed of nothing else for weeks—had fantasized about nothing else but Adam returning to Chelmford and telling her that he loved her. But this . . . this was too much. Marriage? A betrothal ring? How could she accept a ring from him? Loving him as she did, it would be torture to be with him day after day and know he did not love her as she loved him.

Pulling her hands free, she walked some distance away from him and stood staring out at the distant village, at the mill, and at the mill pond. When Adam approached, Marianne felt rather than heard him.

Somehow, he had only to be near her for her better judgment to give way to her senses—senses that longed for his touch, for his kiss. Therefore, when he stepped close behind her and circled her waist with his strong arms, she could not resist the temptation to lean back against him, her head resting upon his chest.

"You deserve better than me," he said, surprising her with the humility of his words. You deserve a man who is not so jaded, a man who is kinder, more selfless, more thoughtful of others."

Marianne turned then, breaking free of his embrace, and looked up into his face. "Adam Jenson, I will not allow you to say those things. You are a good man. A wonderful man. And lest you think you can keep a secret in a village the size of Chelmford, allow me to inform you that it is common knowledge that you personally escorted Bob Quimby's two boys to their aunt in Matlock, and that you bought her a cottage so the three of them could live together in comfort. Furthermore—"

He put his finger across her lips to silence her protests. "I heard what you said to me that day we sat by the fire in your inglenook, and though I was furious with you at the time for pointing out my shortcomings, I know now that you were right."

"But—"

"From now on I shall take a much more active interest in the mill and the villagers. Especially since I have decided that Chelmford is to be my home. It is here I wish to live and rear my children. But only," he whispered, the husky sound of his voice sending shivers of delight throughout Marianne's entire body, "if you agree to be their mother."

"Adam, I—"

"Shhh," he said.

Without asking permission, Adam lifted her hand and placed the beautiful ring on her finger; then, while Marianne waited, her heart in her throat, he slipped his arm around her waist and drew her close against his chest. "My love," he said, the words so sweet she closed

her eyes to savor their magic, "will you take a chance on a man whose first thirty-one years were spent thinking of no one but himself? A man who promises to devote the next thirty to showing you how much he loves you?"

"Only thirty?" she asked. "The way I love you, that will not be nearly enough time."

"Marianne. My sweet Marianne. I am the luckiest man in the world."

When she drew a ragged breath to contradict him, Adam bent his head and claimed her lips, holding her so close that she felt the rhythm of his heart beating against her breasts. With the feel of his strong arms enfolding her, and the warmth of his kisses upon her mouth, claiming her as his own and demanding a response she was all too willing to give, Marianne thought her own heart might burst inside her from sheer happiness.

"Well," he said at last, "what say you, Miss McCord? Will you marry me."

"Actually," Marianne replied, "it isn't McCord after all. It is Wilson. My mother was, indeed, married to my father, so I am not someone's natural—"

Adam stopped her by the simple expedient of covering her mouth with his own. After a kiss that sent delicious sensations all the way to her toes, he lifted his head, the passion in his eyes telling their own story. "What I want to know—what I must know this very moment—is will you allow me to make you Lady Jenson?"

"Yes, please," Marianne said. "And the sooner the better, for I find I am quite impatient to be your wife."

"Now, that," Adam said, the devil dancing in his eyes,

"is the answer I wanted to hear, for I *know* how impatient I am to be your husband."

"Until then," she said, slipping her flattened palms up over his broad shoulders, then around to the nape of his neck, "today is my birthday, and I should like a gift that only you can give me."

Adam's voice was not quite steady. "A birthday gift? Only name it, my sweet, and it is yours."

"I hoped you would say that." Smiling, Marianne lifted her face to his, her parted lips unknowingly provocative. "Would you mind very much kissing me again?"

Adam laughed aloud, then he crushed her soft, willing body against his. "Believe me, my love, there is nothing I would like better. Nothing at all."

## ABOUT THE AUTHOR

Martha Kirkland lives with her family in Georgia. She is the author of six Zebra Regency romances and is currently working on her seventh, *His Lordship's Swan,* which will be published in November 2000. Martha loves hearing from readers, and you may write to her c/o Zebra Books. Please include a self-addressed stamped envelope if you wish a response.

# BOOK YOUR PLACE ON OUR WEBSITE AND MAKE THE READING CONNECTION!

We've created a customized website just for our very special readers, where you can get the inside scoop on everything that's going on with Zebra, Pinnacle and Kensington books.

When you come online, you'll have the exciting opportunity to:

- View covers of upcoming books
- Read sample chapters
- Learn about our future publishing schedule (listed by publication month *and author*)
- Find out when your favorite authors will be visiting a city near you
- Search for and order backlist books from our online catalog
- Check out author bios and background information
- Send e-mail to your favorite authors
- Meet the Kensington staff online
- Join us in weekly chats with authors, readers and other guests
- Get writing guidelines
- AND MUCH MORE!

**Visit our website at
http://www.zebrabooks.com**

# More Zebra Regency Romances

# Enjoy *Savage Destiny*
## A Romantic Series from
# Rosanne Bittner

__#1: **Sweet Prairie Passion**          $5.99US/$6.99CAN
      0-8217-5342-8

__#2: **Ride the Free Wind Passion**     $5.99US/$6.99CAN
      0-8217-5343-6

__#3: **River of Love**                  $5.99US/$6.99CAN
      0-8217-5344-4

__#4: **Embrace the Wild Land**          $5.99US/$7.50CAN
      0-8217-5413-0

__#7: **Eagle's Song**                   $5.99US/$6.99CAN
      0-8217-5326-6

---

Call toll free **1-888-345-BOOK** to order by phone or use this coupon to order by mail.

Name _____
Address _____
City _____ State _____ Zip _____
Please send me the books I have checked above.
I am enclosing                                    $_____
Plus postage and handling*                        $_____
Sales tax (in New York and Tennessee)             $_____
Total amount enclosed                             $_____
*Add $2.50 for the first book and $.50 for each additional book.
Send check or money order (no cash or CODs) to:
**Kensington Publishing Corp., 850 Third Avenue, New York, NY 10022**
Prices and Numbers subject to change without notice.
All orders subject to availability.
Check out our website at **www.kensingtonbooks.com**

# Put a Little Romance in Your Life With
# Hannah Howell

| | |
|---|---|
| __Highland Destiny<br>0-8217-5921-3 | $5.99US/$7.50CAN |
| __Highland Honor<br>0-8217-6095-5 | $5.99US/$7.50CAN |
| __Highland Promise<br>0-8217-6254-0 | $5.99US/$7.50CAN |
| __My Valiant Knight<br>0-8217-5186-7 | $5.50US/$7.00CAN |
| —A Taste of Fire<br>0-8217-5804-7 | $5.99US/$7.50CAN |
| __Wild Roses<br>0-8217-5677-X | $5.99US/$7.50CAN |